MURDER REPLETE...
for now

*Book Three In The
O'Toole/Starker
Murder Mystery Series*

G. A. Cockerham

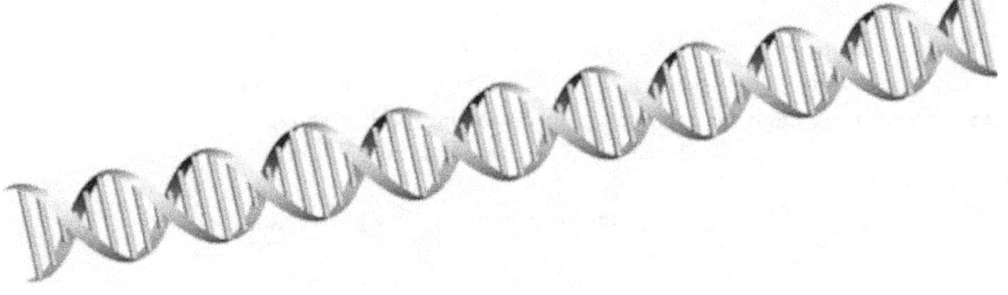

ISBN-13: 97809892408-8-8

ACKNOWLEDGEMENTS

I would not write the O'Toole/Starker series without the technical assistance of my husband Bruce, whose knowledge and experience maintain reality in reference to the law enforcement terms and conditions. Bruce is also my constant source of support and encouragement, both of which keep my mind on mystery and my fingers clicking away at the computer.

Bruce Cockerham is a retired police captain with thirty years' experience in law enforcement. He has worked in patrol, traffic, detectives, SWAT, and administration, and also worked as an academy instructor. He trained with the FBI as a counter sniper and is a graduate of both the California Command College and the FBI National Academy. He holds a BA from Whitworth University and an MDiv from San Francisco theological seminary. He currently serves with the Curry County Sheriff's Office as a civil-enforcement deputy.

Last year, to my delight, I was introduced to Forensic DNA expert Camilla Green. Camilla's professional expertise and consultation have helped to provide an exciting dose of forensic mystery.

My volunteer position for the Curry County Sheriff's Office has afforded me the opportunity to meet many of the fine men and women whose daily work keeps the rest of us safe. Adult Parole & Probation Deputy Dona Dotson kindly lent her expertise to provide accuracy to the parole and probation references.

One of the compliments I often receive about the O'Toole/Starker murder mysteries relates to the humor within the books. Michael "Mick" Espinoza, retired Captain with the Curry County Sheriff's Office, shared a few details of one of the many incidents in which he was involved. I must admit that due to Captain Espinoza's accounting being quite brief, I've heavily embellished the incident to provide one of the humorous encounters within the story.

My sincere thanks to all of you for contributing toward making *Murder Replete… for now* a great read!

Table of Contents

Chapter 1

That's right, officers. Carefully cut the noose so as not to disturb my knot. You won't find fingerprints, and you're thinking that noose may give you a lead. But it won't tell you anything. I put too much planning into this for me to make a stupid mistake. Standing here motionless I can barely contain myself as the excitement of reliving it all washes over me, knowing you have no idea I'm here amongst this magnificent cover of trees. This corpse will be your next cold case and I'm replete, for now.

The call came in shortly after the workday had begun for Detectives Patty O'Toole and Rick Starker. Rick looked up as Patty jotted something down on a notepad while listening to the caller. She then motioned to her partner that they had to leave. "We've got a body at the rest stop north of town," she said after ending the call. "A tourist stopped to give her dog a break and it wandered into the woods and started barking. She found the dog staring up at a man hanging from a tree limb."

Rick stood up, touched his gun out of habit, and followed Patty out the door, leaving a half-eaten doughnut on his desk. Doughnuts had been a mainstay for Rick, going back a couple decades when he was a young cop working night shifts for Boston PD. "I was hoping for a quiet day," he said. "I've got filing to do and a report I wanted to complete."

Patty shrugged. "Looks like your schedule's been changed. This will probably take most of the morning. Shall we take your car?"

"You need to ask?" Rick replied with a smile and then wiped a bit of sweat off his brow. "It's only eight in the morning and it's already warm."

"Yeah," Patty said. "I heard on the news this morning that we'll have the Chetco effect today and tomorrow. Supposed to get up into the eighties in Brookings."

"This Chetco effect is still a mystery to me," Rick said as he turned onto Highway 101, the main street through downtown Brookings, known locally as Chetco Avenue. "It's amazing how it can be twenty to twenty-five degrees warmer here than it is in cities only thirty miles away."

Patty agreed. "It has to do with the north-to-south orientation of the Chetco River mouth and the town of Brookings."

"That would explain why the effect is so localized," Rick said. "I was in southern California a few years ago and the Santa Ana winds were a similar phenomenon."

"Yeah, it's pretty nice," Patty said, "and great for families who take their kids upriver to swim when they're not in school. I used to take Becky when she was little. It'll probably be in the nineties today at Loeb Park."

The distance from their office to the rest stop was only a couple of miles, and Rick pulled up to where Officer Burt "Brad" Bradley was standing.

"Looks like Brad and Pete have been busy," Patty said, seeing orange traffic cones at the entrance and around the targeted area.

Rick parked the car. The two detectives got out and took gloves, cloth booties, and disposable crime-scene coveralls out of the trunk and then walked over to where Brad was standing with a roll of CS tape in his hand.

"Hey, Brad," Patty greeted. "What have we got?"

Brad pointed toward an area of the forest. "There's a guy hanging from a rope just a few yards from the parking lot. She found him," he said, nodding toward a woman sitting at one of the picnic tables with a small dog in her arms. "Well, actually it was her dog that found him first. The dog walked off to do its business and began barking. The woman followed after him and found our victim. She's pretty shook up."

"I'll bet she is," Patty said as she slid the booties over her shoes.

Brad continued. "Other than our female witness, there was no one else here when we arrived. I've got a couple reserves coming over to keep the traffic out. I figured you'd want to call Kindle."

"Okay," Patty said as she and Rick started into the area Brad had indicated. "Let the woman know we'll want to talk with her. It'll be another ten minutes or so."

As they entered the forest the detectives saw a middle-aged man hanging by a rope from the limb of a large pine tree. Flex cuffs secured his feet, and his hands which were behind his back. Patty looked at the ground under the victim before walking to the large tree trunk while Rick took photos of the victim. "These leaves are going to make it difficult to find prints," she said, "and it appears as though someone or something was placed here on the ground. Not much blood in the general area nor on his clothes, suggesting he may have been wounded or killed someplace else before he was hanged."

Rick took photos as he circled the body, including the areas to which Patty was pointing, and then lowered the camera to shoot photos of the ground. "We need rakes to help bag leaves and anything that could have been dropped. Maybe the blood we see belongs to more than just our victim."

"I'll let Brad know," Patty said. She walked back to the parking lot where she found Brad and Pete stringing up the CS tape.

"How far do you want this?" Brad asked.

Patty looked around. "Twenty-five yards in every direction. We're going to need a couple of rakes, and I need you to take the air temperature here under the tree and log it in with the time."

Brad nodded. "I'll ask one of the reserves to help out. Are you and Rick going to use the rakes or do you want Pete and me to take care of it?"

"Why don't you and Pete do it? Go slowly and take photos of anything you find such as footprints, impressions in the soil, or something the responsible may have dropped."

Rick walked out of the forest and over to Patty. "I've got all the photos I need until Ted Kindle arrives. I'll get a knife out of the trunk for cutting the rope."

Patty tapped the number into her phone for Sheriff's Deputy Ted Kindle, Curry County's only deputy coroner.

Ted answered on the first ring. "Hey, Patty, I heard the call on the radio and I'm ten minutes away."

"Thanks, Ted. The victim was hanged by a noose. We'll take the body down after you've had a chance to inspect him."

"We going to need a ladder?" Ted asked.

"No. Part of the benefit of having a six-foot three-inch partner is his reach. The victim is hanging just a few inches off the ground and Rick says he can easily cut the rope."

"Okay. This requires a medical examiner so I'll call Doc Martin and find out whether her schedule will accommodate our victim."

"She'll probably want the body brought to her," Patty said. "I'll notify the funeral director and give him a heads-up."

After finishing her call with Ted, Patty called the funeral home and was talking with the director when Ted pulled into the parking lot. He parked and stood next to his car slipping on the standard CS coveralls, booties, and gloves. He took a moment to look around, noticing the woman sitting at the picnic table with her dog, and then walked over to Patty. "This your only witness?"

Patty nodded. "The only one here when Brad and Pete arrived."

Wrong, Detective O'Toole. I saw that woman and her dog arrive. I wondered how long it would take before you all showed up. Thanks to her dog, I didn't have to wait long. It's been a while since I've seen you, Deputy Coroner Kindle. They need you to confirm no life left in my victim. And that's all you'll find. It was so easy. He practically hanged himself, leaving little time for me to enjoy his anguish. Not a problem, though, as the real fun has just begun. It won't take long before this becomes just another cold case in a back-room file cabinet.

Ted followed Patty and Rick a few yards into the forest and then slowly walked around the victim, looking carefully for any sign of trauma in addition to the victim's neck. "Nothing to see from this angle. We'll need to get him down for me to take a good look at his head. I'll get a body bag out of the car."

Patty nodded and called out to Pete as he wrapped CS tape around a nearby tree. "Can you give us a hand here?"

"Sure," Pete said.

Ted pulled a wallet out of the man's back pocket and handed it to Patty, who opened it up. "Jonas Sorenson with a Brookings address," she said. "I'm not aware of any missing persons reports. Are you, Rick?"

"No, which could mean that he lived alone and didn't work. When we get back, I'll put him in the computer and see if we can find a relative."

Pete walked over to where Ted was holding the body bag. "Let's pull this up over him," Ted said, "and then the two of us can hold him while Rick cuts the rope. When he's free, we'll carry him over to the walkway and put him down on the CS tarp, where I can get a better look at his head."

Rick handed the camera to Patty, reached up, and carefully cut through the side of the rope, keeping the knot undisturbed. "This is interesting rope," he said as Ted and Pete lowered the victim to the ground.

Patty looked at the rope and agreed. "We should probably have Hal Thompson look at it. I'm sure that during his search-and-rescue career he's had to study rope. Let's bring in Hal for a look before we send it off for a complete examination."

"I need some pictures of this," Ted said to Rick, pointing to the gash on the victim's head. "He was probably knocked out long enough for the responsible to position the noose, throw the rope over the limb, and pull him up."

"If that's the case," Patty said, "the responsible thought this through before bringing the victim out here. With his hands and feet tied, the victim couldn't have done anything about the noose even if he came to during the time he was being strung up. Once he was hanged, he'd have been rendered unconscious within twelve or thirteen seconds and died within minutes after that."

"I agree with you, Patty," Ted said. "Certainly appears to be well organized and premeditated."

Patty looked at Ted. "Any idea how long he's been dead?"

"Let me take his body temperature and I might be able to give you a rough estimate."

Rick carefully dropped the piece of rope into an evidence bag. "I'm thinking, Patty, that I should inspect the tree limb prior to our removing the rest of the rope."

Patty nodded and looked at Ted. "Guess we'll need that ladder after all."

"If you're done with me here," Pete offered, "I'll borrow one from Fire and bring it over. Give me twenty minutes."

"Thanks, Pete," Patty said and turned her attention back to the deceased.

"What do you think he was hit with?" she asked Ted.

"That's a question for Doc Martin. She's expecting the victim to be delivered late today or tomorrow morning. Were you able to get hold of the funeral home director?"

"Yes. He's got a driver who should show up here soon to pick up our victim and take him to Medford for the doc."

Ted turned to leave. "Well, there's nothing more I can do here. I'll head north. Let me know if Doc Martin identifies a possible weapon."

"Will do," Patty said. "I'm going to call Hal and find out when he can take a look at our rope. We'll stick around until Rick's had a chance to take photos of the limb where the rope's rubbed against it."

Patty called Hal's number and listened to his voicemail message. "This is Hal Thompson with the Curry County Sheriff's Office. Leave a message and I'll get back with you when I can."

After leaving a brief message, Patty looked again at the woman sitting quietly with her dog and then spoke to Rick. "Pete will be back with the ladder soon. I'll go talk to our witness."

Rick nodded and then looked up to see a hearse pull into the rest area.

The driver, a middle-aged man, stepped out and pointed to the body bag lying on the path. "The director said you've got a body for me to pick up. That him?"

"It is," Rick said. "I'll help you."

Patty saw the hearse enter the area as she approached the woman sitting with her dog. "Hello, ma'am. I'm Detective O'Toole. May I have your name?"

"Hello, Detective. I'm Cindy Salyard."

Patty noticed the pale complexion of the woman and, from the redness around her nose and eyes, assumed she'd been crying. "I'm sorry you found the deceased. Can you tell me what time you arrived and walk me through your actions after leaving the car?"

"Well," she said, "I'm from Cave Junction and was just driving up the coast for something to do. I've stopped here before to let Toby, my dog, out to walk and relieve himself. We were only here a couple of minutes when Toby started barking. He doesn't usually do that so I figured he probably found a squirrel or a deer, and I waited a minute, figuring the animal would run away and he'd stop barking. But he didn't stop, so I got out of the car and followed him to that tree. That's when I saw the man hanging from the rope."

Patty listened as the woman spoke while petting her dog's head and periodically wiping her nose with the tissue she held. "Thank you, Miss Salyard. I know this is difficult for you, and I appreciate your helping us out. Do you remember what time it was when you and Toby arrived here at the rest stop?"

The distraught woman looked down at the ground as though to find an answer to Patty's questions. "Well, I don't remember checking the time when we got here, but we left Cave Junction at six-thirty this morning and this was our first stop. So it must have been about eight."

"That's good information, Miss Salyard. I need to ask: did you walk up to the body or touch it?"

"Oh, no. I grabbed Toby and hurried back to my car. This is all very sad, Detective. Do you think he hanged himself?"

"We don't know what happened. That's all the questions I have." Patty looked up and caught Brad's attention, signaling him to join her with the witness. "This is Officer Bradley. He'll write down your name and contact information in the event we need to talk again with you. Thank you for your time."

Patty joined Rick as Pete drove up in a pickup truck with a ladder in the back. "Matt Horn was at the station," he said, "and let me use his truck when I told him why I needed the ladder."

Pete and Rick carried the ladder to the tree where they leaned it up against the branch with the rope around it. Rick climbed up far enough to be able to look over the top of the limb and took several photos. "There are deep grooves where the rope is wrapped around this limb, but there are additional, lighter grooves as well."

"Does it look like the rope simply moved due to the weight?" Patty asked.

"We'll want forensic confirmation," Rick said, "but it looks to me like the lighter markings were made by the rope being wrapped around the limb without any weight and then released. Like practice throws."

"Goes along with the appearance of being organized and premeditated," Patty said.

"I agree," Rick said. "This killing was planned."

Rick climbed down and helped Pete place the ladder in the back of the truck. He then turned to Patty. "Ready for me to remove the rope?"

"Ready," she said and then started off toward their car. "I'll get a large evidence bag for you." Her cell phone rang, and she saw on caller ID that it was Hal Thompson. "Hey, Hal," she answered.

"Hi, Patty. So you've got a piece of rope you want me to look at?"

"We do. It was used to hang a victim we found this morning at the Brookings rest stop across from Harris Beach State Park. Both Rick and I find it to be kind of unusual so, knowing you're the local expert on such things, we want you to take a look."

"Sure, Patty," Hal said. "I'm in Gold Beach for the next couple of days. Can you have it brought to me?"

"No problem, Hal. You'll have it this afternoon."

"Great. I should be able to get back with you before noon tomorrow."

Patty brought the evidence bag to Rick and filled him in on Hal's call. "There's not much more we can do here. I'll ask Pete to drive our rope sample up north to Hal. Then let's go back to the office and I'll brief the LT on what we've done. Brad and Pete will work on raking up the ground cover."

Rick looked at his watch. "Works for me. It's eleven o'clock so I may have time to finish one of my reports before lunch."

On the way back to the office, Patty's cell phone rang and caller ID showed that it was her mother. "Detective O'Toole," Patty answered, knowing her mother loved it when Patty mentioned her rank.

"Detective O'Toole, this is your mother. Anything exciting happening in Brookings today?"

"Well, Mom, you'll read about it in the paper. Rick and I just finished up on a call at the rest stop across from Harris Beach State Park. A man's body was found there."

"Wow!" Maggie replied. "Was it murder? Do you have a suspect?"

"That's all I can tell you right now, Mom. Did you need something?"

"No, not really. I just wanted you to know that Bill and I are going on a weekend cruise on the Columbia."

"That sounds like fun, Mom. When do you plan to leave?"

"Tomorrow," Maggie said.

"That soon? For how long have you had this trip planned?"

"Well, we only just made the reservations. Because of Bill's gambling reputation, we get great deals for cruising as long as we make the trip soon after booking it. On the large cruise ships it usually means the cruise line has a poker tournament scheduled, or they're attempting to fill up the ship."

"Will you be putting Oscar in a kennel?"

"No. Our neighbor Tom offered to keep him for us. He and Oscar get along well together, so Bill and I feel much better about leaving him than we would if we used a kennel. At seven months old our little Dachshund still acts very much like a puppy and wants to be held."

"You're fortunate," Patty replied, "to be able to leave so quickly and not be confined to travelling only during an annual vacation. And to have a neighbor to take care of Oscar."

"You're right, Patty. We are fortunate. Now, getting back to your case. We'll be gone a few days so I won't be able to read about it in the paper. I'll have to rely on emails from you as the details unfold."

"Nothing's going to happen quickly, Mom. I'll let you know when you get back if there's any new information I can share."

"Well, okay, dear. I'll see you when we return."

Patty quickly responded before her mother hung up. "I need some additional information about your cruise, Mom. Let me call you this evening when I have time to talk."

"Okay, dear. I'll be home packing and look forward to your call. Bye now."

"Bye, Mom."

Rick smiled. "Another cruise. Your mom and Bill sure know how to enjoy life."

"They do. I wasn't sure about Bill when they first started dating, him being a professional gambler and all. But I've come to like him and appreciate how he cares for Mom."

Rick turned into the police department parking lot and looked again at his watch. "I've been yearning lately for a bacon cheeseburger. Let me know when you're up to it."

"Sure. We should have time today after I talk with the LT. Got a place in mind?"

"Well, I can think of three, depending upon how much time we'll have."

"Okay," Patty said as they walked into the building. "I'll need to check messages so let's plan on about noon."

Rick walked to his desk as Patty continued on down the hall to the lieutenant's office. The venetian blinds were open, allowing him to see Patty as she walked up to his door. "Come in, O'Toole. Tell me about the body that was found."

"Thanks, LT," Patty said, taking a seat across the desk from him. "The victim has a gash on his head bad enough to render him unconscious, so we're figuring the responsible was able to hang him before the man came to, if he regained consciousness at all prior to his death."

"When will Doc Martin see him?" asked the lieutenant.

"He's being driven over to Medford today and the doc's expecting him."

"You find anything unusual?"

"Well, it might be unusual," Patty said. "Neither Rick nor I recognize the kind of rope that was used, so Hal's agreed to take a look at it. It might also be a bit unusual that the victim's hands and feet were confined with flex cuffs."

The lieutenant nodded. "Not what your ordinary citizen would use." He looked down at his desk, paused, and then looked back at Patty. "Any witnesses?"

"There was a woman at the rest stop whose dog found the victim. She called it in. No one else was there when Brad and Pete arrived. I spoke with the woman and she hadn't seen anyone prior to her dog discovering the victim."

"How do you plan to continue?" the lieutenant asked.

"Brad and Pete are raking up ground cover that we'll send to the lab. We're hoping Hal can tell us something useful about the rope, and we'll get a report from Doc Martin."

The lieutenant quietly nodded in approval.

"There's one more thing, LT. Rick found skinned areas on the branch where the rope was tied, suggesting that our responsible was out there practicing with the rope before he hanged our victim."

"That's good work on the part of you and Rick. You'll have reporters calling before the end of the day. You might want to ask them to request that we be contacted by anyone who drove through the rest stop last night or this morning and saw anything out of the ordinary."

"Will do," Patty said as she stood up and left his office for her own.

Rick looked up from his file as Patty walked in. "Ready for lunch?"

Patty smiled. "Sure. We'll get there before the noon crowd."

CHAPTER 2

At the restaurant Patty and Rick placed their orders. Rick had a skeptical look on his face. "You're generally eating salad," he said. "What's different today?"

Patty shrugged. "No reason. I just love a cheeseburger now and then, and our work this morning has made me very hungry."

Rick laughed. "A lot of people would find this morning's work to cause a loss of appetite. No one can ever accuse you of being squeamish."

"I was when I was younger," Patty said. "I remember clearly an incident in my biology class. Did you ever have to dissect a fetal pig?"

"We did," Rick said.

"Well, we were given the pig and told to use rubber bands on all four legs to tie it down before using the scalpel. I was having a difficult time just tying the little thing down when a rubber band let loose and the end of the pig's foot, I think it was the toenail, went flying across the room. It shook me up so much that I walked up to the instructor and let him know I couldn't do the exercise. He said that I'd fail the class if I didn't continue. I walked out and, though I didn't fail, he did give me a D."

Rick raised his eyebrows. "I guess a lot has changed since then."

"Yeah, after seventeen years this job has a way of doing that. I look at a case like this morning's as an opportunity to give our victim some justice by finding his murderer."

Rick nodded. "You and I think alike on that, Patty. Let's hope we're successful."

As the detectives were finishing up lunch, their radios crackled. It was Dispatch. Someone in Agness reported an attempted burglary by a man running around nude. One sheriff's deputy had responded to the call and now requested backup. The other deputies, including the marine deputy, were all north on Highway 101 at Humbug Mountain, where a landslide had caused a big rig to overturn. Gold Beach PD was tied up too. One officer was in a court trial and the other's vehicle was out of action mechanically on Tomcat Hill. There were no available state police troopers on the highway south of the landslide. Learning that no other deputies nor OSP troopers were available, Rick and Patty left the balance of their lunch, started up their unmarked car, and began the half-hour drive north to Gold Beach.

Rick drove while Patty called in their intent to provide backup. Then she spoke to Rick. "I sure hope the deputy is able to take this guy down quickly so we don't have to drive all the way there."

"That would be nice," Rick agreed. "That stretch of road from Gold Beach to Agness was, last time I drove it, pretty broken up at several places, making for a very slow pace. It may only be thirty-five miles but it's going to take us close to an hour."

"It's still like that," Patty said. "Agness is an interesting destination, being on the Rogue River. I love taking the jet boats to get there, but driving is another story. Did you know they didn't have electricity until the nineteen-sixties?"

"I didn't," Rick said, "but I can understand a for-profit company not wanting to put in the miles of electric lines to a remote location. It wouldn't be cost-effective for the stockholders. If it weren't for electric cooperatives, there might be a lot of rural areas still in the dark."

"That's what I understand," Patty agreed.

Rick drove out of Gold Beach and was turning onto Jerry's Flat Road toward Agness when their radios crackled.

"I'm in Old Town and in pursuit on foot," said Deputy Stewart. "The suspect is heading toward the river. It's pretty low right now. He may try to cross. I have PC for a burglary arrest."

Patty responded. "This is Detectives O'Toole and Starker. Probable cause will do it for us. We've just turned onto Jerry's Flat Road and we'll get there as soon as possible."

Rick turned on the siren and lit up the car but couldn't drive much faster than any other motorist due to the condition of the road and the hairpin curves.

"He's in the river trying to get across," reported the deputy. "He's having a hard time due to the strong current. I think it best for me to keep an eye on him from the bank." A while later the radio came alive again. "Looks like this guy may be stuck. He's holding onto a rock to keep from going downriver. We're going to have to throw him a rope when you get here."

"Okay," Patty replied. "We'll ask for one at the lodge."

Upon arriving, Rick and Patty pulled into the parking area of one of two lodges on the river, where they saw a group of tourists standing on the bank looking down. Across the river was another group of tourists enjoying the excitement from Singing Springs Resort.

"I can hear the tourists now," Rick said. "'We enjoyed a great meal, shopped for gifts, and then watched a naked man try to cross the Rogue River while fleeing the police.'"

Patty smiled and opened the car door. "Gotta keep them coming back. Let's see where he's at, and then get the rope if it's still needed."

From the river bank the detectives could see a nude male standing in the river holding onto a rock. Deputy Stewart was standing at the foot of the river bank.

"What do you think, Rick?" Patty asked.

"Looks like it will be best," he said, "if we attempt to rescue him from the other side. Let Stewart know we'll get a rope and meet up with him."

Patty notified the deputy, and she and Rick were given a rope to use when they inquired at the lodge. They got back in the car and drove the short trip north to the only bridge connecting Old Town Agness with the road out.

Upon reaching the other side, Rick spoke as they got out of the car. "You know we've got to give Deputy Stewart a hard time about this."

Patty looked at Rick and smiled as they started down the path to the river's edge where the deputy stood, keeping an eye on the man in the river still clinging to the rock. He looked up as Rick and Patty approached.

"Hi," Patty said, realizing she'd not previously met the young deputy. "Detectives O'Toole and Starker."

"I'm Deputy Stewart. Steve Stewart," he said.

Rick looked seriously at the young deputy and glanced out at the man clinging to the rock. "Did he take any property with him?"

The deputy looked at the naked man in the river and then back at Rick. "Ah, um, well, I don't think so."

Rick nodded and then with all seriousness asked, "Is he armed?"

The deputy looked again at the guy in the river and then at Rick who was now smiling. "Not according to the woman whose trailer he'd entered when we got the call."

"Good response," Patty said, also smiling. "Before we go in after this guy, I want to talk to him. Don't want him to panic and head downstream."

Rick began preparing the rope as Patty took a couple steps into the water.

"Hello, sir," she called out. "I'm Detective O'Toole. It looks like you're a bit stuck. We're here to help. What's your name?"

The man hesitated and then yelled out to Patty, "Don't come any closer or I'll let go."

"You must be getting awfully cold," she said. "Where are your clothes? We'll get them for you so that you can warm up once we get you out of the water." Patty waited but the man didn't respond.

"I'll go in to get him," Rick said, preparing to secure the rope around his waist.

"I think it would be better if I went in, Rick," Patty said. "If the guy panics after we've got ahold of him, you and Steve will have an easier time pulling me out than Steve and I would pulling you."

"What if he struggles when you get there?" asked the deputy, looking at Patty's five-foot-five frame.

"Oh," Rick said, "she may not be very big, but she can handle him."

"I've got a PFD in the trunk," said the deputy. "I'll get it."

Patty stepped back onto the bank and waited for Deputy Stewart to bring the personal flotation device. Rick secured the rope around her after she'd put on the device. Patty started across the river and called again to the man. "Do you have family here, sir?" The man looked up at Patty but said nothing as she slowly approached. "Do you live here in Agness, sir?"

Patty was close enough now to see that the man was having a hard time holding on. She figured it was more due to the cold since the river was low and not moving too fast.

"Leave me alone," he yelled out as Patty approached the rock.

"I'm just going to help you to the bank," she replied. "I'm thinking that a nice bowl of hot soup might taste pretty good to you about now."

The man looked up at Patty without speaking.

"What do you say?" she asked as she braced herself against the rock and extended her hand toward the man.

He looked at her hand and then looked up at her. "Okay. But I'm afraid to let go of this rock."

"I understand. Let me tell you what I'm going to do. I'm going to take your right arm with my left hand and pull you toward me as you push away from the rock with your left hand," she instructed. "Then I'm going to stand behind you and slide my right arm around your chest so that I can hold onto you as we cross the river. That okay with you?"

"Yeah, I got it. And you'll buy me a bowl of hot soup?"

"You'll get the soup," Patty said. "All you have to do is walk backward, pushing yourself toward me."

The man nodded.

"Hey," Patty said. "Before we do this, I'd like to know who I'm helping. What's your name?"

"Lyle McDonald," the guy said.

"Okay, Lyle. Let's go," Patty said as she slowly gripped the man's arm above his hand.

Rick and Steve held tight to the rope, pulling Patty and Lyle across as they took one step at a time. All was going well until Lyle's feet slipped as she and Lyle stepped into a low spot, causing Patty to also lose her footing. Patty held tightly onto Lyle as she was carried downriver, digging her heels into the gravel bottom until there was no slack left in the rope and she was able to stop.

"We've got you, Patty," Rick yelled. "Come on in."

Patty walked backward about another eight steps when the water shallowed considerably, and she was able to release Lyle so that he could walk the rest of the way on his own. Rick and Steve walked over to take custody of Lyle as he stepped up onto the bank.

Patty took the towel Steve offered. "It's a good thing it's only October. If that water was much colder, I'm not sure I could have held onto our suspect."

"You were great, partner," Rick said. "Steve can take Lyle in, and we'll head back to the office where you can get dried off and changed."

"That suits me fine," Patty said. She then looked up at Steve. "You need to go into Singing Springs Resort and buy a bowl of hot soup to go. He can have it after you've booked him."

Lyle looked at Patty. "Thank you, Officer."

"You're welcome," Patty said. "And it's 'Detective.'"

On their way back to the office, Rick laughed. "Well, that deserves a place in the top funniest calls I've ever been on. It's right up there with the tamale teller."

"It might seem funnier to me when I'm dry and warm. Right now it's hard to laugh," Patty said. "So, what's this about the tamale teller?"

Rick chuckled again as he drove. "A few years before I left Boston, we were called to a local bank. The bank manager called about one of his tellers. Seems the guy was bringing in hot tamales every day and selling them from behind the counter. The bank manager's office was on the second floor, and he only discovered what was going on when he visited the tellers and saw someone at the teller window exchange bills for a tamale."

"That is funny," Patty said. "What did the bank manager expect you to do about it?"

"Well, you know how it is. We get called for a lot of things. The bank manager didn't know what to do and figured we could arrest the guy. I suggested that this was a personnel matter and not something for the police."

"Did you ever learn what happened?" Patty asked.

"I did. I saw the bank manager a few months later and learned that the teller who was fired for selling tamales subsequently sued the bank for discrimination. Claimed he was fired because he was Latino. Might have had some traction in another area of the country, or at another bank, but this bank had a Latin-American charter and ninety-fine percent of the employees were Latino."

Patty smiled. "Just when I think I've heard it all. So, got any more stories from your Boston PD years?"

"More than we have time for now." Rick smiled. "I was hoping to get a couple of reports written this afternoon, but they'll have to wait until tomorrow. You have a busy evening planned?"

Patty looked down at her soaked clothes. "You mean besides cleaning my gun? I need to talk more with my mom about her cruise, and I want to check in with Becky. She's working hard to get her bachelor's degree in three years so that she can go on to veterinarian school."

"Think she'll make it?" Rick asked.

Patty nodded. "No doubt in my mind. She spends all her waking hours either in the classroom or doing homework. I greatly admire her ability to think about what she wants, set a goal, and then remain focused until it comes to fruition. Leaves little time, however, for mother-daughter talks."

"Well," Rick said, "I wonder where Becky gets that drive?"

Patty looked over at Rick, who glanced her way with a big smile. "I know," she said. Then, as Rick pulled into the office parking lot, "I'm going to brief the LT on the Agness incident. You heading for home?"

"Right after I check my messages," Rick said. "You want to start off tomorrow with a summary of what we've got on the hanging?"

"That would be good. Let's find out as much as we can about our victim while we're waiting for forensics on the rope and body."

Rick parked, and he and Patty walked into their building and down the hall. Rick turned into the break room while Patty continued to the lieutenant's office.

"Come on in, O'Toole," he said. Then, noticing how wet Patty was, "I heard you drove to Agness as backup. Decide to go swimming while you were there?"

"Not exactly." She explained the incident and why she was chosen to go into the river.

The lieutenant smiled slightly. "That the first time you and Detective Starker met Deputy Stewart?"

"It was, and we worked well together."

"Seems it was good work by all three of you. It's helpful to have friends in other agencies."

"Yes, sir."

"Now," said the lieutenant, "I expect you should go home and get comfortable for the evening."

Patty stood to leave. "Thanks, LT. It'll be nice to get out of these damp clothes. See you tomorrow."

CHAPTER 3

Rick was at his desk when Patty walked in. He had a bacon-topped maple bar in his left hand and a pencil in his right.

"It's not even eight o'clock yet," Patty said. "Trying to get caught up on your reports?"

Rick responded without looking up. "Always. I know that with this murder investigation, time for anything else will be scarce." Then, pointing to the white bag on his desk, "There's a chocolate old-fashion in there if you want it."

Patty smiled as she opened the bakery bag and took out the chocolate-covered pastry. "Yum-m-m. You know, Rick, you could be the law-enforcement poster man for pastries and validate the association of cops with doughnuts."

Rick swallowed. "Let me tell you. There was a time when I and a lot of other cops were really grateful for doughnut shops. They were the only food places open at 3:00 A.M. for a cop working graveyard."

Patty smiled. "You no longer work night shifts."

Rick raised his maple bar to his mouth, ready to eat another bite. "I know. Now I eat them solely because I want to. You talk to the LT about your dip in the Rogue?"

"I did, and he said it was good work on the part of all three of us. He also said that it's helpful to have friends in other agencies."

Rick looked up at Patty. "I sure agree with that. An agency that thinks they can do it all on their own is going to miss something big."

Patty nodded. "Like Claire and Skylar's murder. Boston should have used the ViCAP system early on instead of attempting to keep the investigation completely in house."

"I agree," Rick said. "The Violent Criminal Apprehension Program was developed for cases like mine. I'll always be grateful to you for suggesting we work on the case, and to the LT for allowing us to investigate. There will never be for me what some refer to as 'closure' but knowing, after the sentencing, that their killer would no longer be walking around free was like lifting a great weight from my shoulders."

"I could tell it made a difference, Rick. I also find that each year that passes since your tragic loss opens you up a little more. It's like you are adapting to life without your wife and daughter."

Rick put his pencil down. "I work every day at adapting, Patty. And it's the hardest thing I've ever done."

There was a pause in the conversation when the phone rang on Patty's desk. "Detective O'Toole. Hey, Brad. Okay. Starker and I will be right there. Don't let anyone touch anything and keep people off the premises."

Patty hung up and looked up at Rick who'd already closed his report file and stood ready to leave. "Last night someone broke into Weed World, stole quite a bit of cash, and cleaned out their supply under the front counter."

"I thought that store had an alarm," Rick said.

Patty spoke as she and Rick walked out of the building. "It does for the front door and windows. The burglar gained access through the wall."

"The wall?" Rick asked as he and Patty got into his unmarked.

"Yep," Patty said. "Seems whoever burglarized the place got in through the wall between the store and the empty space behind it."

"This I gotta see," Rick said.

Pulling up to the burglarized store, the detectives saw Pete at the front door. Before leaving the car, Rick opened the trunk and pulled out a couple pair of gloves and cloth booties for himself and Patty. The detectives put the gloves on and climbed the stairs to the front door where Pete stood. "Brad's inside," he said. Pete Chekowsky and Burt Bradley had worked together for the past ten years and seemed to know instinctively who would do what at a crime scene.

Walking into the store, Patty and Rick looked around. There were three walls with shelves on which sat jars of different sizes holding the store product in various forms. The check-out counter was over a large glass case about two feet from the fourth wall, allowing enough room for whomever sold the merchandise to stand. In the wall behind the counter was a large hole.

"What have we got, Brad?" Patty asked.

Brad pointed through the hole in the wall. "That's a commercial space for rent that should be entered through the front door on the opposite side of this building. According to the landlord, the space has been available for about three months. Someone broke into that space, drilled holes in this shared wall, and then connected the dots with a hand saw. They came in, emptied the cash register, and took everything from under this counter."

"No motion lights?" Rick asked.

"The owner's got a small fortune invested in alarms on the front door and all windows. There's no back door. He's got infrared motion sensors that would pick up anyone parking in front of the store, climbing the stairs to the door, and entering this room through the front door or windows. There's nothing in place to catch someone moving behind the counter."

Patty and Rick glanced at each other. "That strongly suggests that the burglar knew the security set-up," Patty said.

"Yep," said Rick. "I hope the owner keeps a list of clientele."

"And will cooperate with us," Patty added.

"Okay, Brad," Patty said. "Rick and I'll go around and take a look at the adjoining space and point of entry. You and Pete need to tape off the area, including the adjoining space and its front parking spaces. "Have any of the surrounding business owners been over yet to ask what happened?"

"Only the manicurist across the street. She starts work at eight and saw first the owner and then us show up this morning. She was concerned since she's often there by herself this early."

Patty glanced across the street and saw the salon. The business had two large windows with the blinds pulled down. "We'll talk with her when we get done with the room next door. Take down the name and number of anyone else who asks about the CS tape."

"Will do," Brad said. "Being in here's like watching one of the many training films we've seen. There's pot in every shape and form you can imagine. Makes me wonder how there can possibly be enough users to take it all in when you consider that this is only one of six stores here in Brookings."

"It's difficult to understand how they are all able to make a living at it," Patty said. "Though, from what I've read, the market may be experiencing a glut. Could be one or two stores will have to close soon."

Brad shrugged. "Can't say I'd be sad about that. Our kids deserve better than to grow up in a town with a bunch of pot stores."

Rick had been listening to the conversation and before stepping out the front door, he remarked, "I don't think our kids were a top priority for those who voted to legalize pot. In fact, I don't think they were considered at all."

The detectives walked around the strip center which held the pot store, a couple other businesses, and the empty commercial space that shared a common back wall with the pot store. The door easily opened when Rick pushed on it. "Looks like someone broke the lock," he said. Then, taking a closer look at the doorknob, "It's been a while since I've seen this."

"The type of lock?" Patty asked.

"No, the manner in which the lock was broken. Whoever broke in used a Channellock, a pliers that leaves a unique imprint."

Patty looked at the grooves in the doorknob. "That's new to me."

Still with cloth booties over their shoes, they walked into the room.

Rick walked directly to the back wall. "It's just a big, empty, relatively clean space, except for this hole in the wall and the dust from these two large pieces of sheetrock and studs."

"Seems the burglar was pretty careful," Patty said, "except for what looks like a partial footprint here where the dust lay. In addition to the doorknob, he may also have left prints on the piece of sheetrock he took out, and where he grabbed the edges of the hole in order to climb through. Why don't you take photos? I'll ask Brad and Pete to dust for prints here when they're done next door, and to bring in the sheetrock and studs as evidence."

You're making me angry, Detectives, spending time on some pot-shop burglary when you've got a murder to solve. Forty-eight hours into the case and you've probably heard from the medical examiner. She'll send off some DNA swabs, but they'll find nothing on me. I know how to play this game. How long before you give up? I'm guessing two weeks and I'll declare myself the winner, again.

After Rick completed his photos, the detectives drove back to the office. Patty's desk phone began ringing before she got to her desk. She picked up the receiver. "Detective O'Toole."

"Hey, Patty, it's Hal. Is this a good time to talk with you about the rope?"

"It is, Hal. Rick and I just walked in. I'll put you on speakerphone. Go ahead."

"Well, you two were observant in finding the rope a bit unique. It's called Goldline and was used a lot before the mid-seventies."

"How was it used?" Rick asked.

"Shortly after World War II, ropes were made with nylon, including Goldline. The Goldline rope used by the military was colored green. Goldline was also used by climbers because of the increased safety factor."

"What made it safer?" Rick asked.

"Goldline rope is made by twisting fibers of material into yarns which are then twisted around each other in the opposite direction to get strands which are again twisted around each other to make the final rope. The twisting makes it stronger and lighter."

"What happened in the seventies?" Patty asked.

"The Goldline, along with other rope brands, was very stiff, causing it to turn easily with weight at the end of the rope and it would spin the climber around when the rope reversed itself. In the 1970s ropes began being manufactured to be longer, stronger, and skinnier. Depending upon the type of climbing you did, the newer ropes were the preferred choice of many."

"Type of climbing?" Rick asked.

"Right. If you were going to climb where you needed resistance to abrasion, you might be willing to pay a lot more than if you needed rope for a climbing gym."

"I never thought about the complexities of rope," Patty said. "It must be helpful information to you."

"More than helpful. Knowing about rope has been crucial on more than one occasion when we've had to rescue someone off the side of one of our hundred-foot bluffs or pull them out of the ocean."

"Hal, you never cease to amaze me," Patty said. "You're a walking encyclopedia about search-and-rescue tools and practices. You, the sheriff, and other members of your team have saved a lot of lives, and we're lucky to have you here in the county."

"We've got a good team, Patty, and most of them are volunteers who continue to educate themselves for the purpose of saving lives."

"I've just added another reason why I live here," Rick laughed. "I think this is reason number eight or nine."

"Well," Hal said, "glad I could help out. Hope you catch the responsible on the hanging."

"Thanks, Hal," Patty said.

"Anytime, Detective O'Toole."

After hanging up the phone, Patty looked at her notes. "What do you think, Rick?"

"Well, the rope can probably be found on the internet or at some military surplus stores. Could be the responsible had the rope for years, too, before using it on our victim."

Patty agreed. "Do you think you could check online in Crescent City for an Army/Navy-type surplus store that carries Goldline?"

"I'll do that before lunch," Rick said.

Before Rick could say any more Patty's cell phone rang. "It's Doc Martin," she said, reading the number on caller ID. "Hello, Doc."

"Hi, Patty. How are you and Becky doing?"

"We're fine, Doc. Thanks for asking. Becky's doing great in school. How are things with you?"

"Well, there's not enough money in the budget to hire another medical examiner so I guess I'm keeping up. Frank and I have a vacation planned next month to celebrate our twenty-fifth anniversary. I'm keeping my fingers crossed that we have a cold snap so that everyone will just stay home until I get back."

"Sounds like a plan," Patty said.

"So, about your victim. The gashes in his head would have rendered him unconscious, but being hanged is what killed him, and he would have died within seconds."

"Gashes?" Patty asked.

"Yes. There are several small holes within a relatively tight area."

"Any idea what kind of weapon was used?"

"That's where it gets interesting, Patty. It would take more than one or two of these small gashes, if they were made at different times, to knock your victim unconscious. I'm guessing someone used a bag in which there were several small metal objects and swung it at your victim's head. The combined force would have been much greater than the effect of any single object."

"Are you able to guess, based upon the shapes of the gashes, what the metal objects may have been?"

"That determination will take more than my examination, and I've sent photos and tissue samples to the state crime lab. They're not as backed up as they were a couple years ago, but it could still take two or three weeks."

"Thanks, Doc," Patty said. "Your explanation helps in that we know we're not looking for a single object. How long before we hear on the DNA?"

"Well, you're probably looking at about the same time frame as your results on the tissue samples. Wish I could be of more help, but you and Rick will figure this out."

"I'll pass your vote of confidence on to Rick. Thanks again and take care."

"You take care too, Patty."

CHAPTER 4

Patty looked up at Rick as he worked on a report. "Got time for me to fill you in on Doc's findings?"

"I've got about ten minutes left on this report."

"Okay. I'll go fill in the LT on both the Doc's and Hal's information."

The lieutenant was at his desk when Patty walked down the hall.

"Come in, O'Toole."

"Thanks, LT," Patty said as she took a seat across the desk. "We just heard from Doc Martin and she says the gash on our victim's head isn't from a single instrument. It appears to be several small punctures close together. She suggests that the weapon used was a bag full of several metal objects but can't make out the possible shape of each. She's sent photos and tissue samples to the state lab along with blood samples for DNA identification."

The lieutenant nodded without saying anything. Patty knew this was his way of processing information and she waited quietly for his response.

"If we find out what was in the bag, we may have a better idea as to who our killer is."

"You mean like a theme?" Patty asked.

"Exactly. Have you heard anything yet from Hal?"

"He called a little while ago. Said the rope is called Goldline. The premier rope for climbers at one time. It's available at several online websites but Rick is checking out the Army/Navy surplus store in Crescent City before checking the online businesses."

"Good work," said the lieutenant. "Keep me posted."

Patty got up to leave. "Will do, LT."

Rick was just finishing up a call when Patty returned to her desk. "See you at five," he said before hanging up.

"You got a date tonight?" Patty asked.

"No, I'm going fishing tomorrow with Sam, a buddy of mine. We'll meet at five for breakfast."

"That's early. Only one place I know is open at that time," Patty said.

"Yep," Rick said with a smile. "Oceanside Diner. Opens at 4:30 for the commercial fishermen. They serve a great breakfast including grilled oysters."

"Sam from around here?"

"No, he lives up north. Travels up and down the coast a couple times a year in his RV, staying at his favorite parks and fishing a few of our many rivers. He's parked at the Driftwood RV Park for a couple weeks while here in Brookings. Then he'll travel up the coast to the Indian Creek RV in Gold Beach. When he leaves Gold Beach, he'll head north to the Winchester Bay Resort at the Salmon Harbor Marina."

"I'm familiar with all of those parks," Patty said, "and he can't go wrong with any of them. Seems like a nice way to live. Something I'd like to do when I retire."

"I'm with you on that," Rick said.

"Does he also drive the coast on his return south?"

"No," said Rick. "He drives over to Sutherlin where he has family. One of his cousins owns Sutherlin Drug."

"I've been there," said Patty. "I stopped in once to pick up some aspirin and was impressed by all the beautiful gift items they carry."

Rick smiled. "Sam calls it 'Oregon's hidden gem.'"

"So, what are you fishing for?" Patty asked.

"Ling cod and rockfish are about it at this time of year. We wouldn't be out at all if the weather wasn't so mild."

"We're enjoying a beautiful fall," Patty said. "I could get used to sixty degrees through November. Hope you and your buddy catch your limit. As I recall, you did pretty well during salmon season."

Rick grinned. "I did, and I've been reading up on them to better understand the controversy about salmon and the Columbia River dams. There are written records about the uses for salmon in different areas of the world going back more than a thousand years. They've played a key role in keeping not only humans but many animal species alive."

"I frequently read about their role in the Columbia River-related conflict," Patty said. "Some folks want to remove the dams, claiming they contribute to the decline of the fish."

"Yeah. It's very controversial. So much so that about thirty percent of our electric bill goes to salmon-related lawsuits and maintenance programs."

"Thirty percent?" Patty repeated.

"At least," Rick said. "And the interesting part of it all is that Pacific salmon spend very little of their lives in the river. They're in the ocean the rest of the time and the ocean temperature can have a great impact on the salmon's longevity. They gain well over 90% of their weight at sea and return to their home streams to spawn and die."

"Do you think the salmon are overfished?" Patty asked.

"Well," Rick said, "I'm not an expert on the subject, but there are those who believe overfishing and habitat degradation have contributed to the demise of the species. The thing is, their habitat can change every time a tree or large rock falls into the river, or a storm shifts the direction of water."

Patty's cell phone rang. "It's Becky. I need to take this, but I'm interested in hearing more about the salmon. Hey, Bec. What's up?"

"Hi, Mom. Just wanted to let you know I'll be home late tonight. Josh wants to take me out to dinner to celebrate his 4.0 second-quarter GPA."

"Now that's something to celebrate," Patty said. "Tell Josh congratulations for me. Where's he taking you?"

"He wouldn't tell me. Said it's a surprise and asked that I take a study night off since we've not gone out for dinner in a while."

"Well," Patty said, "I hope you both have a wonderful time. It's been close to six months now that you two have been dating. You like him a lot, Becky, don't you?"

"I do, Mom. And I like that we both want to complete our education before making our relationship permanent."

"You're both smart kids, Becky. Have a nice time tonight. I'll be asleep when you get in."

"I know, Mom. I'll knock on your bedroom door to let you know when I'm home."

"I've always appreciated your doing that, Bec. Even when it was an order."

Becky laughed, but before either of them could continue, Patty's desk phone rang. "Got to go, Bec. I'll call later. Love you."

"You too, Mom."

Patty answered the phone. "Detective O'Toole."

"Patty, it's Brad. Pete and I spoke with Weed World about a list of customers over the past three months and they said no problem. But there is a problem in that the only list they have is that of credit-card users, and most of their sales are cash. We've got about twenty-five transactions listed and twelve are from three customers."

"Hold on, Brad," Patty said, and she filled Rick in on the call.

Rick nodded. "Let's run them all. See if anyone has a record."

"You hear that, Brad?" Patty asked.

"Got it," he said. "I'll let you know what we find."

Patty looked at the files on her desk and then up at Rick. "We may have to set this case aside for now," she said. "Wait for the state lab to get back to us on that piece of sheetrock."

Rick nodded. "It would be great if they found prints to send to AFIS."

"It would be," Patty said, "but then AFIS won't be much use unless our responsible is already in the system."

"I'm betting he or she is," Rick said. "This was a well-planned-out burglary. Not just some pothead looking to get high."

"Well, we should know within the next four to six weeks," Patty said. "My understanding is that the backlog of the past couple of years has been cleared."

Rick laughed. "So we can call it the Automated Fingerprint Information

System again instead of the Automated Fingerprints In a Couple Years System?"

Patty smiled. "That's what I've been told. Changing the subject, I don't want to come in over the weekend so I'm going to finish this report now. Hope you pull in a lot of fish tomorrow."

"Thanks. So do I."

CHAPTER 5

Both detectives were at their desks by mid-morning Monday. "I called the Army/Navy surplus store in Crescent City," Rick said, "and they do carry Goldline rope. I've got an appointment with the owner scheduled this afternoon to go over his records on anyone who's purchased the rope within the past couple of years. Want to come along?"

"No, I'm having a late lunch with my mom and Bill. She sent a text a little while ago saying she and Bill have something they need to tell me."

Rick smiled. "You thinking he popped the big question over the weekend?"

Patty shook her head. "No. Mom sounded serious. Kind of sad."

"I hope they are both okay," Rick said.

"Yeah, me too."

"I've got a tight schedule today," Rick said, "and I'm leaving early for Crescent City so that I can stop at Del Norte Office Supply before my appointment."

"Will you pick something up for me?" Patty asked.

"Sure. What do you need?"

"They carry a great selection of holiday goodies including Elf-On-The-Shelf hot chocolate which is something I used to serve Becky when she was a kid. She can enjoy it with Josh and tell him about the elf game."

Rick put his jacket on and touched his gun. "That elf thing is foreign to me but someone there will help me with it. Hope your lunch goes well."

"Thanks, Rick. I do too. I'll let you know this afternoon."

Rick left, and Patty took care of a couple calls before leaving for lunch. At the restaurant she found her mom and Bill already seated.

Bill stood as Patty walked to their table. "Hi, Patty. We're glad you could join us."

"Of course," Patty said as she sat down. "Mom's call this morning sounded serious. Is everything okay with you two?"

"The waitress is on her way over," Maggie said. "Let's order before we talk."

Orders were taken and waters set down for each of them. All was quiet, and Patty saw her mom take Bill's hand before he spoke.

"Patty, I've been diagnosed with cancer."

Patty sat quietly processing what she'd just heard. "Cancer? When? What kind?"

"It's prostate cancer," Bill said. "I had a PSA test completed a few months ago and another last week. Three tests over the past twelve months show an increase. The doctor gave me the news at my appointment last week. I'll have surgery on Wednesday."

"I'm so sorry," Patty said. "This is pretty sudden. Why didn't they detect it sooner?"

"Well, I went five years without the test because the physician I was seeing at the time told me I was too old to need them anymore, given I had no prior problems. That physician moved out of the area and my new doctor required the test as part of his initial new patient workup. He said I should be tested every year regardless of age. Turns out he's right."

"But why surgery?" Patty asked. "I thought most men develop prostate cancer and can live with it for decades."

Maggie nodded. "That was my understanding too, Patty. There are slow-growing cancers, but Bill's is not of that type. His best chance is to have the prostate removed, and we want whatever will give him the greatest number of remaining years."

"Of course," Patty said. "Where are you going for the surgery?"

"Medford," Bill said. "I've researched the surgeon and feel very confident in his skills and credentials."

"What can I do?" Patty asked.

"There's really nothing you can do now," Maggie said. "This is new for us, so we'll take it one day at a time after the surgery. We don't know what effect it will have for a while on Bill's ability to get around, so we'll probably need more visits from you at our place rather than us going to yours."

"Bec and I will both visit and take turns at bringing meals so that you can take care of Bill. We can take Oscar too."

"Thank you, dear," Maggie said. "The meals will be great, but we'll leave Oscar with Tom. He's always asking if he can dogsit for us. I think he enjoys his brief visits with us as much as he enjoys taking care of Oscar. He's pretty shy and seems to spend a lot of time alone at home. I think that Oscar cheers him up."

"It's good you have someone you trust to care for him," Patty said. "May I let Rick know?"

"Definitely," Bill replied. "It should be a reminder to him to get an annual PSA test. I plan to tell every man in our lives that, regardless of age, he should ask for the test annually. It could save a life."

Their meals were served, and Patty filled them in on Becky's developing relationship with Josh. After lunch she looked at her mom and Bill as tears pooled in her eyes.

"We're going to be okay, Patty," Maggie said. "Bill has an expert surgeon and will recover as expected. We're already discussing the cruise we want to take next spring. We plan to enjoy many more years together and will carry on with our lives once we rid Bill of this horrible disease."

"I love you, Mom," Patty said with her arms around her mother's neck. Then turning to Bill, she gave him a quick hug. "And you too, Bill."

"We love you too, Patty," Maggie said. "Now back to work. Did you catch that murderer yet?"

Patty shook her head. "Not yet, Mom. But you'll be the second to know when we do. Right after the LT."

Patty returned to her office, where she found Rick working with a cookie in one hand and a pen in the other. A small white bakery bag sat on the edge of his desk. Rick swallowed as Patty walked in. He pointed first to a brown bag on her desk and then to the white bakery bag. "There's two cans of that elf's powdered hot chocolate in that bag and a few cookies in this one. Help yourself. You were right about all the interesting food and gifts. I've never had a need to look around when I've gone in for office supplies."

"Having just finished lunch, I'll pass on the cookie, but thanks for buying the chocolate. What do I owe you?"

"Nothing. I'll let you buy me lunch sometime. How'd lunch go with your mom and Bill?"

Patty sat down at her desk and looked up at Rick. "It's sad news, Rick. Bill has cancer."

"Cancer!" Rick exclaimed. "I'm so sorry. What kind? What's his prognosis?"

Patty leaned back in her chair and exhaled. "It's prostate cancer. He's scheduled for surgery in Medford on Wednesday."

Rick paused before responding. "Why so sudden?"

"Bill's doctor has recommended it. Bill has also received a second opinion. He has a good friend, a retired urologist to whom Bill sent his test results. After reviewing the charts, his friend advised him to have the surgery. He'll only be in the hospital a day and a half, and my mom will stay over in Medford and then bring him home."

"You know," Rick said, "I guess I always figured PSA tests were only for older guys. I've never had a doctor suggest one to me, but then I'm only forty-three."

"Bill says men should have the test regardless of age," Patty said. "I think it's like many health care areas. We have to be our own best advocate. You need to request the test on your annual doctor visit."

Rick raised his eyebrows. "I don't have an annual doctor visit."

Patty leaned forward at her desk. "Then make an appointment. It's important."

Rick nodded. "I will. I'm real sorry about Bill."

"Thanks, Rick. So, what did you find out about Goldline?"

CHAPTER 6

"Two people in the past few months have purchased Goldline rope. One guy, a Michael Rice, lives in Crescent City and the other in Smith River. The salesman I spoke with, who also manages the store, couldn't remember much about either one of them except the guy from Smith River said he needed it for a project. Said he'd been in the Navy where he used the rope for a lot of things. The Crescent City guy used a credit card, so I'll get ahold of him. Smith River used cash."

"There's probably a slim chance," said Patty, "that our responsible is one of them, but let's interview the Crescent City guy as soon as possible. I'll let the Del Norte County Sheriff know about the guy from Smith River so that he's aware of the rope connection. Do you have a plan for contacting other surplus stores?"

Rick nodded. "I do. I'm going to contact the Goldline headquarters and get a list of retail stores currently buying Goldline from them. I'll also start calling every Army/Navy surplus store in our area of the country for information on sales of the rope over the past couple of years."

"That's great, Rick. When you're talking with Goldline headquarters, you might also ask if they sell to individuals purchasing small amounts or only to retailers."

Rick made a couple of notes in his file. "Will do. This a good time to go over what we've got so far?"

"It is. Let's start with our victim whose name is Jonas Sorenson, according to the wallet found in his pants pocket, and who was hanged with a Goldline rope from a tree branch in the rest area across from Harris Beach State Park."

"We found rope marks on the tree limb," Rick added, "strongly suggesting the responsible practiced throwing the rope over the limb prior to hanging our victim."

Patty added another notation to the list in her file. "According to our ME, the initial exam suggests our victim was struck on the head with a bag full of small metal objects prior to being hanged. This would have rendered him helpless for a period of time on the ground while the responsible placed the noose around his neck and hoisted him up."

"We have no witnesses," Rick said, "and the woman whose dog found our victim saw no one else in the park while she was there. She said her dog barked only when coming upon the victim, suggesting that there was no one else around her at the time."

"We have no missing persons report," Patty said. "Brad and Pete have been working on the victim's background and may come up with something more for us. We assume our victim didn't work, but an inspection of his home might confirm that. We should soon get the search warrant that I requested yesterday. The judge signed it and someone's bringing it down to us." Patty put her pencil down and stared at her notes. "Who are you, Jonas Sorenson, and why were you killed?"

Rick laid his pencil down and looked up at Patty. "Maybe we'll have something to add to our list after visiting with Mr. Rice."

"Wouldn't that be helpful?" Patty said. "Let's take a ride to Crescent City. Call Michael Rice and ask if we can talk with him in either thirty minutes or an hour and a half from now. If thirty minutes works, we'll leave now for Crescent City and interview him first, then drive to Jonas Sorenson's house. We'll reverse the timing if Mr. Rice needs ninety minutes before we arrive."

Rick made the call on his cell phone and was able to talk with Michael

Rice. After finishing the brief conversation, he filled Patty in. "Rice isn't home right now but said he could be in two hours. I told him to expect us."

"Okay. Brad sent a text that our search warrant is in the mail sack at the front desk, so let's head over to Sorenson's now. If we have a little free time between inspecting his house and leaving for Crescent City, I'd like to make a stop at Ambiance By The Sea so that I can buy a fortieth-birthday gift for my cousin."

"I know where that is," said Rick, "but I've never been inside."

Patty looked a little puzzled. "Where do you go to buy unique gifts?"

"I don't," Rick said.

"You've never purchased something for someone else in the five years you've been here in Brookings?"

"Well, now that you put it that way, yeah, I've purchased a couple books from Forecastle Books. They have a great selection by local authors including a couple of great murder mysteries with an Oregon coast setting."

"Ambiance By The Sea carries those murder mysteries too. So does Brookings Harbor Visitor Center and the Driftwood RV Park."

Rick shrugged. "Just never had a reason."

"Well, I think you should check out our local shops, Detective Starker. Having a supply of unique gift shops is like having tools in your toolbelt. Never know when you might need one."

Rick smiled at Patty. "So gift shops are the tools in your toolbelt? And you wanted me to believe you went into Sutherlin Drug for aspirin. I'm always learning something new about you, Detective O'Toole."

Patty smiled back as she and Rick left the office. "No need for both cars if you want to drive."

Rick felt for his gun, dangled the keys, and followed his lead detective out the door.

Pulling up to Jonas Sorenson's house they saw nothing unusual about it or the neighborhood. It was a small house a block from the grammar school. The house on the north side of Sorenson's looked well cared-for while the house on the opposite side of the street appeared to be in great need of attention. A common neighborhood dichotomy of sorts.

Rick knocked on the front door. "Police. Anyone home? We have a search warrant." He waited thirty seconds, repeated the announcement, and when no one answered, he used the key they'd found in the victim's pocket. The detectives donned their booties and gloves, walked in, and viewed the house layout. The kitchen was opposite the front door, a living room to the right, and bedrooms and a bathroom down the hall to the left. After a quick walkthrough to confirm they were alone, they entered the kitchen.

Patty opened the dishwasher while Rick looked into the refrigerator. "No dishes in the sink and everything in the dishwasher has its own space. The forks, spoons, and knives are kept separated."

"The contents of the refrigerator suggest he lived alone. It's a typical array of foods, a six-pack of Coke, four beers, a jar of peanut butter, condiments, and pickles. The freezer is full of TV dinners and a couple of steaks."

Patty walked down the hall looking into each room. "The bedrooms are as neat as the kitchen, and the medicine cabinet has a couple over-the-counter drugs including three bottles of Pepto-Bismol. It appears our Mr. Sorenson had experienced some stress in his life. I'll take a look at the closets."

Before Patty could look further, Rick called out from the living room. "In here, Patty."

Patty walked in and saw Rick with a framed photo in his hand. He held out the photo, and as Patty took it, she stared at a photo of Mr. Sorenson in full uniform. Patty looked up at Rick. "He was a cop!"

CHAPTER 7

Patty placed the photo in an evidence bag and opened the drawers of the desk on which had sat Mr. Sorenson's photo. "Arcadia, Louisiana," she said, holding up a pay stub. "Must be where his pension came from. We need to find out when he retired and whether he has family there."

"Arcadia's a long way from Brookings," Rick said. "What could have brought him out here?"

"That's what we're going to find out," Patty said. "Write on the receipt that we're taking the framed photo and pension check slip. The kitchen table is probably a good place to leave the copy of our warrant."

"Done," Rick said. "Now let's lock this place up and learn why Mr. Rice needed Goldline rope."

"We've got about forty minutes," Patty said, "giving me time to purchase my cousin's gift and still make the appointment. While you drive, I'll call the Crescent City police chief and let him know why we're there."

Immediately after crossing the Oregon/California border, Rick followed the orange cones leading motorists off the highway and into the drivethrough entrance for the California Department of Food and Agriculture inspection station. As they slowed to a stop, a woman standing outside a small office smiled at Rick. "Got any fresh fruit?"

Rick turned to Patty who shook her head no. He then looked back at the woman inspector. "No," he claimed, to which she responded, "Have a nice day."

Rick pulled back onto the highway. "CA tax money at its best."

Patty laughed. "It does make you wonder about the cost-benefit analysis that someone must periodically update. Though I have heard that some people do voluntarily turn their fresh fruit over to the inspectors and that this has resulted at times in finding unwanted pests. On another topic, did you see all the spinning lawn ornaments at the house across from the bug station?" Patty asked.

"I've noticed it before," Rick said. "Why?"

"Because that's McMillen's Art Gallery and Gift Shop. Another tool in my toolbelt of unique gifts."

Rick smiled. "Thanks for the tip. I should have no problem finding stores the next time I need a unique gift."

Rick turned off the highway onto a side street in Crescent City, not far from the grammar school. "This should be interesting," he said. "I've never spoken to someone about rope."

"Me neither," Patty said, "and I'm hoping we'll leave with more information than we have now. I'll take the lead and you jump in anytime."

The detectives arrived at Michael Rice's home and walked up the steps. Almost immediately after the doorbell rang, the front door was opened by a boy who appeared to be about six. Running up behind him was a younger girl followed closely by a man.

Patty and Rick showed their badges. "Mr. Rice?" Patty asked.

"Michael," said the young man. "And these are my children, Kaden and Sophie."

"We're Detectives O'Toole and Starker."

"Come in," said Rice as he backed up, giving the detectives room to walk through the door. "When Detective Starker called, he said you wanted to talk about the Goldline rope I bought."

"Thank you," said Patty as she and Rick followed the young dad into his living room.

Rice pointed out a couple of chairs where the detectives could sit, and then gave his attention to the two children. "You two can sit on the couch if you can do so quietly or go play in your room." Both children chose the couch, and Michael Rice sat down across from the detectives. "What can I help you with?"

"We're following up on a case," Patty said, "and want to learn more about the various uses of Goldline rope. We've learned that you recently purchased some of the rope at the Army/Navy surplus store. Can you tell us for what use you bought it?"

Rice stood up and walked over to a large picture window where he pulled back the curtains and pointed toward the back yard. "For that," he said, smiling.

Patty and Rick stepped over to the window and stood looking at a home-made zip line with about ten steps leading up to the start of the line. At the other end was a tent-like structure filled three feet deep with small, colorful plastic balls.

"Can I show the police how it works, Dad?" asked the young boy.

"Sure," Rice said. "Hold onto the railing when you go up the stairs."

"Me too," squealed the little girl.

"Not this time," her dad said. "This time you stay with me and watch your big brother."

Patty smiled as she saw the young boy climb the stairs, take hold of the handle his dad had made on the rope's end, and push off. He hung on for the twenty- to thirty-foot ride, letting go over the high bed of plastic balls. "That's pretty neat," she said to Rice.

"Sure is," said Rick. "Looks like every young kid's dream."

"It was mine,' said Rice. "I grew up with few store-bought toys and used my imagination for entertainment. The zip line is something I'd always wanted to build."

There was a pause in the conversation before Patty spoke up. "Why Gold-line?

"Before I had the responsibility of raising kids, I did a fair amount of ama-teur rock climbing. Goldline was one of the ropes I used for certain climbs."

"Makes sense," Rick said. "You bought this at the local surplus store. Do you know of any others that carry it?"

Rice shook his head. "I don't, and I'd suggest that very few surplus stores carry Goldline anymore. My finding it at the store here was a bit of an accident. I'd gone in looking for a tent and just happened upon the rope. If you're looking for someone who sells Goldline rope, I suggest you look at stores that carry climbing gear."

Rick nodded. "Thanks for the tip."

"And thank you for your time," Patty said as she and Rick stood up to leave.

"No problem, Detectives. I hope you find whatever or whomever you're after."

Patty and Rick climbed into their unmarked and noticed a Crescent City police car down the street. Patty waved and the driver of the car drove on down the road. "Good to know we had backup if needed," she said.

"I agree and I'm glad we didn't need it. Rice seemed to know what he was talking about with respect to where we might find the rope. So I'll change the course of my plan and concentrate on stores where climbing equipment rather than surplus is sold."

"You might start with Oregon, California, and Louisiana," Patty said. "We don't yet know if the responsible knew our victim before he moved out here."

"I'll do that," Rick said as he drove north on Highway 101, back toward Brookings.

"So, tell me another Boston story." After a few moments of silence, Patty asked again. "You have another one?"

Rick chuckled. "I've got lots of other ones. I'm just thinking of one you might appreciate. Okay. Here's one. So a call comes in about a dead guy in one of the local bars, and my beat partner Ben and I take the call. We walk into the bar and find a guy lying on the floor next to a bar stool. His head, cushioned by a folded bar towel, is bleeding, and he's lying in a pool of blood. The bartender and about seven other guys in the bar are carrying on like this was an everyday occurrence."

Patty enjoyed Rick's stories, in part because it seemed that as soon as he started talking about Boston, his accent became twice as thick as it normally was. "What time of day was it?" she asked.

"Between five-thirty and six P.M. The guys that were there would regularly drop in after work and shoot the breeze for an hour before going home to their wives and families. So anyway, I feel the guy's carotid while Ben calls Fire and Ambulance. Far as I can tell, the guy's dead, but we don't know why or how he came to have fallen off the bench and hit his head. I look around the room and holler out, 'Nobody leaves until I say so!'" Rick began to smile and paused.

"So what happened next?"

Now Rick had a hard time talking without laughing. "The seven guys sitting at the bar all became quite giddy as they stepped over the dead guy one by one and lined up at the one public telephone in the bar. Each called his wife explaining that the police would not let him go home for at least another hour. They were a pretty happy group of guys as they returned to their seats, again stepping over the body lying on the floor, and ordered more drinks."

"That is funny," Patty said, laughing. "What was the reason for the guy's fall?"

"He'd come into the bar drunk, sat down, and said, 'Gimme a bromo.' The bartender said he turned around to fill the order and turned back to find the guy gone. He'd fallen off the stool and hit his head. That's when the bartender called 911, put a bar towel under the guy's head, and then carried on as usual."

"Wow," Patty said. "Wouldn't you think at least one of those guys would have checked to see if their mate on the floor needed help getting up?"

"No, I think they all knew he wasn't going to be getting up and figured there was nothing they could do about the situation except order another round."

"We don't have enough of a population here to create hilarious stories like your calls in Boston."

"Sure you do," said Rick. "You've had a couple of funny bank robbery episodes. There was that woman who wore flip-flops and the guy who escaped in a taxi and stopped for lunch before leaving town. My Boston friends would love to hear both of those stories."

"I guess we have enjoyed a good laugh or two."

Rick's story took about the same amount of time to tell as the trip back to Brookings from Crescent City. Just prior to crossing the Chetco River Bridge, he turned right, then turned again under the bridge and toward the harbor. "Let's get some lunch before returning to the office. We may not find time once we get busy again."

"Sounds good to me," Patty said.

I'm in the car behind you, Detectives, and I know where you're going. I'll sit here in the parking lot while you eat. I don't know why you stopped at that house in Crescent City, but I did see the black-and-white. That's why I drove right by you and waited on the next block. Did you really think your kind could hurt me and not pay for your crime? I look at your pictures every day. You and the others taped to my wall like targets. All of you thinking you could outsmart me. But I'll not be caught. You'll be just another police department with a cold case I'll read about in the paper some morning as I sip on a fresh cup of coffee, enjoying the fact that I've outwitted you all!

* * *

After lunch Patty and Rick returned to their station. Patty stopped in to see the lieutenant, and Rick walked to his desk to make phone calls.

"Come in, O'Toole," said the lieutenant as Patty started to knock on his door. "Where are you and Rick with the hanging?"

Patty sat down across from the lieutenant at his desk. "Rick and I just returned from Crescent City where we spoke with one of two men who've bought Goldline rope within the past two years. He seems to have had a valid use for the rope and suggested we look at stores that sell mountain-climbing equipment rather than surplus. Rick will start with stores in Oregon, California, and Louisiana.

"Louisiana?" asked the lieutenant.

"Yes, sir. We searched the victim's home and discovered he was a cop in Arcadia, Louisiana. I'll call the Arcadia Police Department when I get back to my desk. Find out how long ago he served and whether anything happened on his watch that may be associated with his death."

"Let me know if you need help with that, O'Toole. Not all agencies are willing to share information. Be your usual polite self and let them know that we'll include them in the flow of information if there's a connection between our murder and their community."

"I will," said Patty. "This case is quickly becoming more and more curious." She stood to leave. "Thanks, LT."

'You're welcome, O'Toole."

When Patty returned to her desk, Rick looked up. "You know, I forgot to ask. Did your mom say whether she and Bill were concerned about taking their weekend trip so close to the date of his surgery?"

"No, the doctor said that it wouldn't hurt. He figured it might do them good to have that time together since Bill's recovery will cause a good three-to-six-month interruption in their regular schedule."

"Well," Rick said, "I hope they were able to relax."

"I don't know about relaxing," Patty said, "but it gave them time to process the diagnosis. It's all just so abrupt!"

Rick nodded and there was a minute of silence between the two before Patty spoke. "I'm going to call the Arcadia PD while you make your calls. Let's plan on going over our notes together in about an hour." Rick nodded and opened his file.

Patty dialed the number and after two rings heard a young woman's voice on the other end of the line. "Arcadia Police Department. May I help you?"

"Yes, thank you. My name is Detective Patty O'Toole and I'd like to talk with Chief Todd."

"Hold on, please, Detective, and I'll find out if he's available."

Patty estimated that she waited less than thirty seconds before hearing the gruff voice of a man now on the line. "This is Chief Todd."

"Chief, I'm Detective Patty O'Toole with the Brookings, Oregon Police Department. We've had a murder here and found in the victim's home a stub from his Arcadia pension check."

"Arcadia's a fairly small town, Detective. Tell me the name of the business and I'll let you know if I knew the man."

"I'm calling you, Chief, because the pension check is from the City of Arcadia. Our victim was a cop."

After a brief pause, Patty spoke again. "His name was Jonas Sorenson. Did you know him?"

Patty heard the chief exhale.

"Oh my God," he said. "Jonas was here twelve years and only retired a few years ago. Said he was going someplace with less stress. How did he die?"

"We don't have confirmation back yet from the state lab, but it appears that he was hit on the head and then hanged from a tree limb in a park that serves as a rest area off the highway. We found the check stub at his house in a desk drawer and a picture of Sorenson in uniform on top of the desk. We found no evidence of a family or connections other than the City of Arcadia."

"Do you have a suspect?" asked the chief.

"We don't and at the moment have no clues. Do you know if Sorenson had any family?"

"Well, he wasn't married," the chief said. "And I don't remember him talking about kids. Seems he might have a brother. That information should be in the personnel file."

"We'll look when we have the file," Patty said. "Do you know of any reason why someone from Arcadia may have wanted to kill Sorenson? Maybe someone from one of his cases?"

"There are certainly those who Sorenson helped put away who may have wished him harm, but I don't think any of them would actually kill him. There is, however, someone who believes he was wronged by Sorenson, but this is just too much of a coincidence."

Patty was now intrigued with the chief's last comment and figured Rick should listen to the explanation. "I'm going to put you on speakerphone, Chief, so that my partner on this case, Detective Starker, can join us."

Rick moved the file he was working on to the corner of his desk and placed a clean tablet in front of him as Patty continued. "Who is this guy who thought he'd been wronged by Sorenson, and what's coincidental about Sorenson's death?"

The chief cleared his throat before speaking. "Five years ago we had a guy apply for an entry-level position. We hired him with an eighteen-month probation period and a dismissal-without-cause clause in his contract. Turned out the guy was a loner and not the team player he proclaimed himself to be in his interviews. There were a couple of minor complaints from other officers, but we kept him on for about nine months until his actions sealed his fate. We had a vehicular fatality in which a young woman died. She was held overnight at the medical examiner's facility in New Orleans. During the twenty-four hours she was there, one of our sergeants who had attended the scene of the accident stopped in to finish some of the details he needed for his report. When he entered the room where the deceased was being held, he found Officer Faires standing next to the table with the cover pulled down off of the victim's head and torso, and his hand on the victim's chest. Faires quickly left when the sergeant walked in and later said the victim was uncovered when he'd arrived and that he was pulling the sheet back up. When asked why he was there at all, he said he figured looking at a dead body would help to desensitize him, making him more useful when responding to future fatalities."

"So what did you do?" Patty asked.

"The sergeant reported the incident back to me and I had him write it up. After receiving the report, I met with my two sergeants and the city attorney. The following day, I called Faires into my office, went over the incident with him, and relieved the officer of his duties."

"How did Sorenson fit into this action?" Patty asked.

"He was the sergeant who wrote up the report."

"Chief, this is Detective Starker. What was Faires' reaction to being let go?"

"Well," said the chief, "surprisingly, he didn't really react. Just quietly stood up, put his coat on, and walked out. We figured he'd accepted that he screwed up."

"So," Patty asked, "what makes Sorenson's murder a coincidence related to Faires' situation?"

The chief paused. "Sorenson was one of the two sergeants I consulted, and both have died."

"How did the other guy die?" Patty asked.

"That's the coincidence, Detective. He was found three years ago hanging from a rope."

Chapter 8

atty and Rick locked eyes with each other before Patty continued the conversation. "Chief, was there an investigation?"

"There was after the fact. Hal Grover had retired with Sorenson about two years prior. We found a suicide note which read that he couldn't live without a purpose in life after retirement. His wife was gone, and he had no kids. Because of the note and with no obvious wounds on the body, we didn't treat the scene as anything other than a suicide.

"Two days later, the coroner called, explaining that he'd found marks on Grover's chest similar to those left by a stun gun."

Rick sighed. "Are you telling us you didn't process the rope or any part of the house?"

"That's what I'm saying, Detective. Hal Grover lived outside the Arcadia city limits in Bienville Parish. We've always been a poor parish, and the sheriff's office didn't have the staff and money to conduct investigations in the manner to which you may be accustomed. The deputies saw the suicide note and figured it was the act of a depressed cop."

"So what about evidence after the ME discovered the stun-gun marks?" Patty asked. "Did they save the rope?"

"I'll have to check on that for you. It's possible one of the deputies locked it up in evidence with us since Grover had been one of ours."

Rick looked up from his notes. "We need all of the information you have in your files, Chief, on both the fired officer and Grover's death. We also need to see Faires' application, background, and personnel file.

"Well, as I recall, there wasn't much, and back then we didn't do pre-employment backgrounds, but I'll send you what we have. As for Grover, you'll want to talk with the detective who handled the case. Marty Rogers. I'll have my assistant get his contact information for you. Marty retired last year but still lives here in Arcadia."

"We'd appreciate the information, Chief," Patty said. "When can you get back to us about any possible evidence your department has on the case?"

"I'll check on that after this call and let you know."

"We'd also like to see everything the Bienville sheriff's office may have. Can you arrange to have that sent to us as well?"

"I'll do what I can, Detective."

"Thanks, Chief," Patty said. "We'll be in touch."

"Detective O'Toole?" the chief asked.

"Yes?"

"There were three people involved in Faires' dismissal. Sergeants Grover and Sorenson, and me. I don't like the odds right now. I'll do everything I can to get you what you need to help catch this guy."

"Thanks again, Chief. We appreciate your help."

After ending the call Patty stood up to walk out of the office. "I need to let the LT know what we've got."

In the lieutenant's office Patty went over the phone call. "It's hard to believe that they'd have been so careless as to assume it was a suicide before the coroner had a chance to look over the body."

The lieutenant nodded. "It is to us, O'Toole, but we're fortunate to have a department of very well-trained officers and two exceptional detectives. Cities like Arcadia, with fewer than three thousand residents, are lucky to have a handful of officers. They can't pay enough to keep younger cops around or afford to provide frequent training programs to those who do stay."

"So you're saying we just work with what we have?"

The lieutenant nodded. "It is what it is. You and Rick have more to go on now than you did before your call with the chief. Talk with the detective who worked the case."

Patty thanked the lieutenant and walked back to the office where Rick was enjoying a doughnut.

"They're in the break room," he said, "if you want one."

"I'm still digesting my lunch," Patty said with a smile. "So, what do we know now that we didn't know before?"

Rick looked at the notes he'd taken during the call. "We know that our victim was one of three people involved in terminating one Morten Faires about five years ago."

"And," Patty said, "we know that a second of those three, Hal Grover, was found hanged in what originally was assumed to be a suicide and subsequently changed by the coroner to a probable homicide."

Rick tapped his pencil on the desk while thinking. "We'll soon know if there was any evidence held from that crime, and we'll receive the contact information for the original detective on the case."

"The LT suggested we get ahold of the Arcadia detective and said that he too thinks the chief has reason to be concerned."

Patty's cell phone rang, and she saw it was from the Arcadia PD. "Detective O'Toole."

"Detective O'Toole, this is Charlotte from the Arcadia Police Department. The chief asked me to call and give you the name and contact information for Marty Rogers."

"Yes, Charlotte. Go ahead."

Patty took the contact information and thanked Charlotte for the call. Before hanging up Charlotte spoke again. "Oh, I almost forgot. Chief told me to tell you that we do have that rope you asked about in our evidence room. Chief says he'll have it preserved for any future testing."

"Thank you again, Charlotte. That's good news."

Rick was shaking his head when Patty hung up the phone. "No telling what they'd have found if more evidence had been located at the scene."

Patty nodded. "I expressed some of the same sentiment to the LT and he reminded me that not every department has the funds for continual training of their officers. Let's call Detective Rogers and learn what we can from him." Patty made the call and had to leave a voicemail. "Mr. Rogers, this is Detectives O'Toole and Starker from the Brookings, Oregon police department. We've had a murder here, and we're interested in talking with you about the death of Hal Grover." Patty left both of her numbers before ending the call and giving her attention back to Rick.

Before they could continue, Patty's cell phone rang, and she glanced at caller ID. "Hey, Brad."

"Hey, Patty. We've got prints on the piece of sheetrock our Weed World burglar removed from the wall and we're running them through AFIS now. We've also got a name Pete found on one of the credit-card receipts of a guy who regularly delivers pizzas to the store. The owner says the delivery guy often engages him in conversation that has included the security system."

Patty laughed. "And I suppose the owner of Weed World explained how it worked?"

"He did."

"Okay," said Patty. "Talk to the owner of the pizza parlor and find out whether this guy was working the night of the burglary and let me know if you get anything on the fingerprints. WIN covers eight western states, so chances are our guy is in the system."

"Will do," Brad said and Patty ended the call.

"WIN?" Rick asked.

"I guess I haven't used that term before," said Patty. "WIN is the Western Identification Network that consists of eight western states sharing one electronic fingerprint database for use in processing criminal and applicant fingerprints. In addition to Oregon, members include Alaska, Idaho, Washington, Montana, Nevada, Utah, and Wyoming. With input from eight different states, our automated fingerprint ID system is far more valuable."

"Being from the east coast I wasn't familiar with that system," Rick said.

"Probably because AFIS is used nationally," Patty said. "A system like this on the East Coast might have helped us in finding the Munchausen Syndrome woman responsible for Claire and Skylar's deaths."

Rick nodded. "It would have. I'm going to let my Boston cop friends know about WIN."

"It's after five and I'm exhausted," Patty said. "Let's start on this again first thing in the morning. Maybe by then I'll have heard from our former Arcadia detective."

"That works for me," Rick said. "I'm waiting on several call-backs from stores that sell Goldline."

* * *

Patty got to the office early the next morning after stopping by the bakery on her way. She set a small bag on Rick's desk, where she saw his message light blinking, and a second bag on hers. While taking off her jacket she glanced at her desk phone, where a bright red number seven was lit up next to the blinking light. With a yellow legal pad on the desk in front of her and pencil in hand, she reached for the receiver when Rick walked in.

"Morning," he said. "What's in the white bag?"

Patty smiled. "Good morning to you too. There's a bacon-topped maple bar in there if you want it."

Rick smiled. "Thanks," he said. "I most definitely do, and I'll need coffee to go with it. Want a cup?"

Patty handed her mug to Rick. "Thanks. When you get back, I'm hoping that between our two phones there will be at least one voicemail to help with our homicide."

Patty was still listening to voicemail messages when Rick placed her coffee on the coaster she kept on her desk. She gave him the thumbs-up sign and then set down the receiver as he was taking the first bite of his bacon-topped bar.

"Before you listen to messages," Patty said, "let me fill you in on what I've got. Detective Rogers has left a couple of time frames for me to call him back. I'd like for you to be part of that call so let's check our calendars for today. My final call was from Brad. They got a hit on the fingerprints and figure they'll have the Weed World burglar in custody before the end of the day."

"Nice to start the day with good news," Rick said. "What are the time frames Rogers gave you?"

"He's available between ten and eleven or after two today. I've got to be in court at ten but I'm open after two. And you?"

"After two works for me. I'd like to spend the morning with call-backs to the climbing stores."

"Okay, I'll let him know we'll call him at two."

"My messages can wait while I finish this," Rick said before taking another bite of his pastry.

Patty took a sip of coffee. "I'll give Brad's message to the LT," she said, standing up. Less than a minute later she returned to her desk. "He wasn't in his office."

"I had five voicemail messages," Rick said, "and three were from store managers all familiar with Goldline. Maybe one of them sold the rope to our responsible."

"While you make calls, I'm reviewing my notes for the court appearance."

A while later Rick hung up the phone and sat back in his chair. Patty looked up from her notes. "Based upon the one-sided conversation I heard, I'd say you struck pay dirt."

"Yes and no," Rick said. "One store is a small mom-and-pop type and they don't have the room nor the budget to carry a lot of products and don't carry Goldline. The manager of another store I called said they carry Goldline but haven't sold any for some time. He's going to get a list of names and contact information for me for those who purchased the rope with credit cards within the past three years. The third guy is a manager of a large chain store. He said they sell a lot of rope and that it would take a few days, but that he could get me a list of the Goldline customers they've had for the past couple of years. So I'll make more calls once I have the information. I feel like I'm fishing for a goldfish from a boat in the ocean. Maybe our call with the detective will give us a little more to go on."

"Hope so," said Patty. "I'm off to court and, with luck, will be back in a couple hours."

* * *

When Patty returned to the office from the courthouse, Rick was on the phone, still calling stores that sold Goldline rope. As she began to sit down, her cell phone rang. "Hey, Brad."

"Hi, Patty. We've got him."

"Where'd you find him?"

"At his home," Brad said. "And guess what we found on his kitchen counter?'

"I give up," Patty said. "What did you find?"

"A Channellock pliers! Bet the lab will match it up to the doorknob our responsible used it on."

"You find any of the cash?" Rick asked.

"He had a brown paper lunch bag with cash in it. About three hundred dollars."

"What did he have to say?" Patty asked.

"Nada. He lawyered up."

Brad informed Patty of the balance of evidence they had to tie up the case.

"Good work, Brad," Patty said. "You might want to tell Mr. Weed World not to share the details of his security system with his customers or the pizza delivery guys."

"Yeah, Pete told him, and Mr. Weed World agreed. He also remembered talking about the fact that he kept a lot of cash at the store due to federal law not allowing pot store owners to open bank accounts. Guess he let it slip where in the store he kept his stash of cash before he moves it to a safe deposit box."

"Okay, Brad. Let me know who's assigned to represent him."

"Will do," Brad replied before hanging up.

Patty left her desk and walked down the hall where she found the lieutenant in his office.

"Come in, O'Toole," he greeted her.

Patty walked in and sat down. "Brad and Pete have the responsible for the Weed World burglary. He wiped down the doorknob and glass case he broke into but didn't think about his prints showing up on the sheetrock around the hole he climbed through."

The lieutenant smiled. "Takes all kinds, O'Toole," he said. "Was he in the system?"

"He was. A couple burglaries up north. In addition to his prints Brad found the guy's Channellock pliers on his kitchen table. We figure it's the same tool he used to bust the doorknob at the point of entry."

"Anything else?"

"There is, LT. Brad found sheetrock debris on jeans and a sweatshirt in the guy's closet, a pair of shoes that match the prints in the dust, and a paper bag full of cash."

"That should seal his fate," said the lieutenant. "Good work."

"Thanks, LT. I'll pass that on to Brad and Pete."

"Got anything else on the homicide?"

"We've got a two o'clock call scheduled with the now-retired detective who worked the case. We'll get as much information from him as we can on the possible suspect and the two victims."

"Hear anything from the state lab on the rope?"

"Not yet. I was told they're no longer backed up, so I expect that means we should hear something soon."

The lieutenant nodded. "Thanks for the update."

"Sure, LT," Patty said as she walked out of the office and back down the hall.

Rick was on the phone when Patty walked into their office. Seeing her return, he looked up. "It's almost two o'clock. Let me give you a little more feedback on my calls before we contact Rogers. Most of them produced no results, however, I did get an interesting response from the owner of a store in New Orleans."

Patty leaned forward onto her desk. "He remembers someone he sold the rope to?"

"No, no one he sold the rope to, however he does remember a guy who came in a few years ago and asked a bunch of questions about Goldline. Said the guy had a piece of the rope and wanted to know more about it, such as how strong it was and whether it held its strength with age. Said his uncle had talked about Goldline when he served in the Navy. The owner would have thought nothing about it except that before leaving the store, the guy asked if the owner thought the rope would make a good noose."

CHAPTER 9

At two o'clock Patty and Rick called the former Arcadia detective.

"Detective Rogers, we're Detectives O'Toole and Starker from Brookings, Oregon. Chief Todd gave us your contact information and suggested we give you a call. Thanks for agreeing to talk with us about the Grover case."

"Sure, Detective. It's been awhile but I'm happy to help if I can. Why do you think my case has anything to do with yours?"

"A few days ago," Patty said, "we found a man hanging from a rope in the rest area associated with our state park here in Brookings. The only identification we could find for the man was a pension check stub from the City of Arcadia where he was a cop."

"Well," said Rogers, "I was with Arcadia for ten years before retiring last year. When did your victim work here and why do you think he's related to the Grover homicide?"

"He retired from Arcadia PD about five years ago. During his last year, he and Sergeant Grover provided the chief with information resulting in the termination of Morten Faires. Our victim's name is Sorenson."

"Jonas Sorenson?"

"Yes," Patty said. She waited through a minute of silence on the other end of the line. "You knew our victim," she said.

"I did. And I'm familiar with the Faires termination that he and Grover were involved with. This is just too weird."

"That's what we're thinking, Detective, and why we need to locate Morten Faires. When's the last time you saw him?"

"Well, I didn't see much of him following the termination. Then, about two or three years ago, I happened to be in the drugstore downtown when Faires walked in. I'm sure he recognized me because he turned around and quickly walked back out the door."

"What can you tell us about the Grover death?" Patty asked.

"The deputies who first caught the call thought it was a suicide. He'd been depressed for a while and they just figured he'd had enough. When the medical examiner told them about the Taser marks, we were all shocked. None of us could think of anyone who'd want to hurt Grover. The sheriff was short-staffed with his detective on leave due to a family illness. He reached out to our chief for help and gave him a copy of his deputies' report. The chief gave me the report and the case. The only evidence retained by the deputies was the rope, and we locked that up in our evidence room. No one had dusted for prints when the body was removed so I had the chair dusted, but it was just too late. Too many people walking in and out of the house and handling the victim. The only prints we found were those of the deputies involved."

"How, exactly, did it appear that he hanged himself?" Patty asked.

"His house has a beam across the living room ceiling. The rope had been thrown over, and the end tied to the beam. A chair was turned on its side under his body."

"Was there a note?" Patty asked.

"Yes, but it was short. Said he had no reason to live."

"How well did you know Faires when he was working during his probationary period?"

Rogers paused. "I didn't know much about him except for what a couple of the other officers told me. They didn't like him. Said he was antisocial and just plain weird. The way I heard it, no one was sorry to see him go."

"Tell us more about what the officers said that resulted in their conclusion that Faires was antisocial and weird."

"I was told that, early on, several of the guys met up for pizza and asked Faires whether he'd been married or had someone special in his life. Faires said no to both parts of the question. When asked if he'd be interested in meeting someone, he just got up and walked away. No yes, no, or maybe. No anger. Just got up and walked away. He sat by himself in one corner of the room while he finished his beer and then left. After a few months he'd earned the reputation of being very antisocial. Not a team player. You'd have to ask the chief about the specific reason Faires was terminated."

"Thanks," said Patty. "Give us a call if you think of anything else that might help."

"Sure," said Rogers. "If Faires is your responsible, there's a good chance he's ours too. Will you keep me informed?"

"We'll let you know if we arrest him," Patty said.

Patty hung up her phone and sat back in her chair. "What do you think?" she asked Rick. "Based upon your Boston experience, tell me your thoughts thus far about Morten Faires."

Rick sat back, laced his fingers together, and lifted his hands to the back of his neck. "My thoughts may change once we have copies of his personnel file from Arcadia, but based solely on what we've learned thus far, here's what I think. First of all, Mr. Faires knew enough to be hired as a cop and, unless his file reads differently, was able to learn the job and operate for several months. Did he go to an academy or have relatives who are cops? The incident with him traveling to the coroner's office and touching the deceased female's chest suggests Mr. Faires has some psychopathic tendencies. He could be a man who sees himself as having superior abilities to those around him. He wants to control himself but has impulsive urges that cause him to act irrationally. He demands control of all situations and quickly escapes if he senses a loss of that ability."

"The chief," Patty said, "told us that Faires didn't react to being terminated. Didn't argue with his explanation. Just walked out."

Rick nodded. "He may have been practicing his need to control the situation by not showing emotion in response to his termination. I would guess he had an idea before the termination that he wouldn't continue at Arcadia PD, so it wasn't a complete surprise."

Brad knocked on the office door and walked in with a file. "We canvassed both sides of the street for one block in both directions from Sorenson's house. Now a good time?"

"Sure," said Patty. "What have you got?"

"Out of eighteen neighbors, only five said they'd spoken with our victim. The general consensus is that Sorenson was a quiet guy. He moved in about three years ago. He lived alone and no one saw anyone visit." Brad looked at his notes. "One neighbor, a Mrs. Brown, said she'd seen a man sitting in his car out front of her house on and off for several days during the past month. She lives three doors down from the deceased."

"She say how long he sat there?" Rick asked.

"Yes. She said he was there for about five hours a day but at different times each day. Said she thought it seemed suspicious but that she didn't call the police because she lives by herself and didn't want to have any trouble with the man."

"Could she describe the car or the man?" Patty asked.

"Brad turned the page on his notebook. "She didn't know the make of the car but said it was a small blue four-door. She couldn't remember anything else about the car except that one taillight was out. She was peeking out her window one evening just as the car was pulling away when she noticed it had only one working light."

"Did she ever see the man leave the car?" Rick asked.

"No," said Brad, "but during the daytime she could see through the passenger window well enough to tell that he was Caucasian and wore jeans."

"Okay, thanks," Patty said.

"I'm not done," said Brad. "I'm sure that one of the neighbors was lying to us when I asked him about Sorenson. Whether he was lying about knowing Sorenson or something else, I don't yet know. But the guy was real nervous."

"What's his name?" Patty asked.

Brad flipped back a couple of pages and dragged his finger down several lines. "Robert Baird. He lives at thirty-four eighty-one."

Patty looked at Rick. "Maybe we should pay him a visit," she said.

Rick nodded. "I've got time if you want to go now."

Patty stood up and before leaving the office with Rick, instructed Brad. "Put his name in the system and find out what we have on him."

Rick and Patty drove back to Sorenson's neighborhood and walked up the front walk of Robert Baird's house. It was one of two houses on the block in bad need of paint and a gardener for the front yard. Rick knocked. Thirty seconds later he knocked again with no response. The blinds on the front windows were drawn, leaving no opportunity for the detectives to look inside. Patty's cell phone rang, and she saw that the call was from Brad.

"Hey, Brad."

"Patty, I ran Baird's name through the system, and he has a record. He's been arrested twice in Josephine County for burglary and did time for both."

"Thanks, Brad," Patty said before hanging up and relaying the message to Rick. "He could have been nervous because he was high, or because of his prior record."

"Or," Rick said, "because he's already committed a crime here for which he's just not been caught."

"Let me talk with the LT," Patty said. "Get his input before we look further into this guy. I'll ask Pete to sit on Baird this evening and let us know when he comes home."

Patty and Rick walked to their car and headed back to the office. "Send out a BOLO on the blue car," Patty said. "Maybe someone will notice a car with only one working taillight."

Back at the office, Rick stopped in at the break room while Patty continued down the hall.

"Come in, O'Toole," said the lieutenant.

"Thanks, LT. I've got more information related to our homicide." The lieutenant nodded and waited for Patty to continue. "Rick and I spoke with the detective who was given the Grover case in Arcadia."

"Grover, the former sergeant with Arcadia PD," said the lieutenant.

"Yes. Seems the deputies who first worked the scene were sure it was a suicide. The sheriff asked Arcadia PD to help out due to the coroner's findings of Taser marks and subsequent change to homicide for cause of death. The sheriff's detective was out on leave so he asked Arcadia for help. The Arcadia chief put then-Detective Rogers on the case."

"Rogers still living in the Arcadia area?" asked the lieutenant.

"He is, and he explained that other than the rope the deputies locked up in the Arcadia PD evidence room, there was no evidence because nothing initially was dusted for prints."

"Did he have any information that was helpful?" asked the lieutenant.

"He was able to provide us with a description of Faires given to him by other Arcadia officers. The guy was a loner and acted without emotion even at times when emoting would have been the natural thing to do. We've asked for a copy of the personnel file on Faires' termination, and that may give us more about his personality."

The lieutenant sat quietly and let Patty continue.

"That's all we have from Rogers, but we do have a little more information on Sorenson. Brad and Pete canvassed the neighborhood and came across one neighbor, an elderly woman, who said she saw a man parked out front of her home several times during the two weeks prior to Sorenson's death. She never saw the man leave the car but could see him well enough during the daylight hours to see that he was Caucasian and wore blue jeans. She said the car was a small blue four-door with a taillight that wasn't working. Rick's putting a BOLO out on it now. There's a second neighbor that Brad described as unusually nervous. Brad was sure the guy was lying to him when he asked if he knew Sorenson."

"You run him through the system?" asked the lieutenant.

"We did. His name's Baird and he served time for a couple burglaries in Josephine County. Rick and I went back to the guy's house a while ago and he wasn't home. I've asked Pete to sit on him and let us know if Baird returns to his house. We don't have enough for a search warrant so I figure the best we can do is catch him at home and hope he lets us in."

The lieutenant shifted positions in his chair, a characteristic that Patty knew as part of her supervisor's thought process. "If this were California and Baird is still on probation, you wouldn't need the warrant. You could go in based solely upon the right-to-search clause in his probation. Baird may know this and keep his house in Oregon for this reason. Confirm whether he's on probation, and have a discussion with his PO." The lieutenant then smiled slightly at Patty. "You're pretty good with talking to people. See if Baird will let you in and keep him occupied as long as you can while Rick looks around. Rick may see something that will help you obtain a search warrant."

"I'll give Rick your suggestion and we can go back to the house when Pete sees the guy return home."

The lieutenant nodded. "Have you been able to locate any relatives of Sorenson? Someone who may have been in his house?"

"Not yet, LT. We've requested his personnel file from the Arcadia chief, and it should arrive with the file on Faires."

"Talk with some of the other officers who worked with Sorenson. One of them may know if he has a close relative. Someone who can tell you if Sorenson owned anything of value that could be fenced on the street."

Patty pulled the small notepad from her pocket and made a couple of notes. "Are you thinking that Baird may have stolen something from Sorenson's home?"

"It's a possibility," said the lieutenant. "Could explain why he was nervous when shown Sorenson's photo and asked about him."

"We'll check on any relatives Sorenson may have had," said Patty. "And I'll have Brad or Pete go back to the neighborhood to ask if anyone's ever seen Baird enter Sorenson's house."

"When they do go back to each neighbor," said the lieutenant, "the question should also be asked as to whether the blue four-door with the non-working taillight was noticed."

"Will do, LT. Thanks for your help."

"Good work, O'Toole," he said as Patty left the room.

Upon returning to her office she saw a napkin and three cookies on the edge of Rick's desk.

"There's more in the break room," he said without looking up.

Patty nodded. "Good to know. I need to contact Brad now."

"I just saw him in the break room," Rick said. "I'll see if he's still there."

Rick started out the door, stepped back, and looked over at Patty. "Sure you don't want a couple of cookies?"

She smiled. "No cookies."

Rick left and came right back in with Brad.

"What's up?" Brad asked.

"When you discovered Baird did time for a couple of Josephine County burglaries, did you notice if he's still on probation?"

Brad looked down at the floor and then back up to Patty. "Now that I think of it, he is."

"Great. I need the name and contact information for his PO."

Brad started out the door. "I've got it on my desk. Anything else?"

"Yes. A couple of things. Is Pete still sitting on Baird?"

"Yes."

"Okay. I need for you to meet him out there and inquire as to whether anyone may have seen Baird visit Sorenson's house. We also need to know if any of the neighbors noticed the small blue car the elderly woman told you about."

"Okay. I'll let Pete know what you need and that I'm on my way."

Not so smart now, are you, Detectives? I've seen your officers talking with neighbors of my victim. You're working hard to find more clues, anything at all. But you won't. This isn't my first rodeo, and I've been honing my skills for years. It's all so entertaining.

Rick looked up at Patty after Brad left the room. "Did the LT suggest we check on whether Baird has a PO?"

"Yes. He knows we can learn a lot about the guy by talking with his PO. He also mentioned the difference between California and Oregon law relating to our ability to use the search clause in the terms of parole and probation. Did your probation terms have such a clause when you were in Boston?"

"They did. Guess it's been too long since I've needed to use it since I didn't think of that. The LT sure knows a lot."

"He does," Patty said. "He's come up with helpful suggestions many times that I never would have thought of."

"Guess that's why he makes the big bucks," Rick said.

"You know, Rick, I'm not sure that his pay is that much more than ours, but he has a lot more responsibility. I think he really loves his work, knowing how much help he is to us with our jobs. He's also a good ambassador for the department, getting along well with the sheriff and other community leaders."

"Definitely one of the good guys," Rick said. "I worked with a few of those in Boston."

Brad walked back in with the contact information for Baird's probation officer. "I've let Pete know what's going on. I'm heading out there now."

"Thanks, Brad," Patty said. Then addressing Rick, "I'll call the PO."

Patty input the number into her cell phone and heard the call picked up after two rings.

"PO Wakely."

"PO Wakely, this is Detective O'Toole from Brookings PD. I'm calling about one of your clients on probation. Last name Baird. This a good time to talk?"

"Sure, Detective. Baird in trouble again?"

"Not sure. We've had a homicide over here, and Baird lives across the street from our victim. One of our officers spoke with him yesterday during a routine neighborhood canvass and reported that he seemed pretty nervous. My officer is certain Baird was lying when he claimed he didn't know the victim other than having seen him a couple of times. We'd like to search the house for personal effects of the victim or rope like the one that was used in his hanging. We know the search clause in Baird's probation would give you the right to go in if he lived in California, but here in Oregon we'll need his permission."

"You going to try talking him into letting you enter?" asked Wakely.

"That's what we want to do. Okay with you?"

"Baird has been a real problem for me, and I'd love nothing more than to have him become your problem for a while, though murder would be a big step from burglary. You and your partner have my blessing to go in if he'll let you. Let me know if you gather enough information for a search warrant. I'd like to search the place with you. We've had several burglaries within the past few weeks and haven't been able to locate any of the stolen items. Maybe he's responsible and has been stashing the stuff in the Brookings house."

Patty gave a thumbs-up sign to Rick. "We've got an officer watching the house now. We'll let you know what we find. Thanks."

"Thank you, Detective. I'd love to see the lowlife locked up again where he belongs."

Patty hung up and looked over at Rick. "It'll be interesting if we find out Baird has something in his possession that belonged to Sorenson."

"It would also be a great break for us on this case," Rick said.

Chapter 10

Patty tapped a key on her cell phone. "I'll let Brad know that having Pete sit on this guy is all we need for now."

"Hey, Patty," Brad said.

"Hi, Brad. Since Pete's sitting on Baird, you don't have to stick around there once you've finished up with your questions to the neighbors. We'll give you a call when Baird is home. We'll want you for backup if he lets us go in."

"Great," he said. "That should give me time for a welfare check several miles up the north bank."

"Something new?" Patty asked.

"No. It's an alcoholic who periodically visits the church in town. She frequently gets mad at her sister, who is also her legal guardian, and refuses to answer the sister's calls. We've been out at her place several times with complaints called in by neighbors about her standing in the front yard screaming. She's a great example of why we need state hospitals again for the mentally ill. Her problems may all be caused by alcohol, but she really should be living in a secure environment where she could get daily physical and mental care."

"No disagreement here," Patty said. "With the growing homeless problem, state governments may decide they'll have to spend the money. Of course, as soon as they do, there will be as many people against state hospitals as there are for them. As soon as some politician brings up the need, you'll have a half-dozen special-interest groups complaining about the government interfering with individual rights.”

“Well, someone’s going to have to do something,” Brad said. “We deal with a lot of so-called homeless who just don’t want to work, but we also have a fair number of residents like this alcoholic woman who cannot, for various reasons, properly care for themselves. They often become victims of theft and abuse by the criminal element. We’re fortunate not to have much of a problem in our county, but it’s one that overwhelms some law enforcement agencies.”

“It’s a big problem,” Patty said. “I hope the woman comes to the door for you.”

“Me too. I’ll get back to you later with what we learn from talking again with Sorenson’s neighbors.”

“Thanks, Brad,” Patty said.

Her cell phone rang, and she glanced at caller ID. “It’s Becky,” she said to Rick before connecting the call. “Hey, Bec. How’s your day going?”

“It’s okay, Mom. Just wanted to touch base with you about Grandma and Bill. Have you heard from them today?”

“I haven’t, Becky. I plan to call later this evening. You want to check in with her now?”

“Sure. Let me try and I’ll call you back.”

“Thanks, Bec. I know Grandma will be pleased to hear from you.”

Rick set his pencil down. “I hope they’re able to focus on their next cruise.”

“Yeah. I do too. I’m pleased that Becky is taking time out from her studies to give her grandma a call.”

“Becky’s a thoughtful person,” Rick said. “Like her mother.”

Patty raised her eyebrows. “That’s kind of you, Rick, but I haven’t been very thoughtful lately. This case is taking every bit of my attention here and at home.”

Rick smiled. “You just have to practice compartmentalization.”

Patty laughed. “Did you make that up?”

“Not at all,” said Rick. “You already know something about how to compartmentalize or you wouldn’t still be on the job. It’s a matter of being able to mentally leave the job at the office when you go home.”

"Well," said Patty, "I did do that as a single mom when Becky was younger. She demanded all my attention when we were home. But with Bec being able to take care of herself and Mom living with Bill, I find myself wanting to work on some cases, like Sorenson's, even in the evening when I'm home. Are you telling me that you don't think about this case once you leave your desk in the evening?"

"You got me there, Patty, and you're right. I've thought of nothing at home but this case. It was a lot easier to compartmentalize when I had Claire and Skylar to go home to."

"So," Patty said, "we both know how to compartmentalize when we choose to do so."

Rick chuckled. "Yep. We do." He sat forward in his chair. "On the topic of Claire and Skylar, I've been asked by a local grief organization to speak at their meeting next week. They assist those who've suffered the death of a child, grandchild, or sibling."

Patty nodded. "Do they want you to talk about your loss?"

"Yes, in part," Rick said. "Their focus at meetings is on loss, grief, and healing. They want me to tell about my loss, and then how I managed to heal to a point of being able to function successfully as a detective."

"I can see," Patty said, "how hearing from someone who survived the death of their loved one would be important for the newly bereaved."

"That's exactly what makes this organization unique," Rick said. "Most of the bereaved attending meetings at this chapter are bereaved parents. Those who are new to their loss hear from others further along who understand what the loss of a child does to one's mind. A common outcome of child loss can be isolation. The bereaved parent feels isolated due to other people's inability to understand. I've heard it expressed that learning that your child has died is like having a hand grenade go off in your head. The Earth spins off its axis and everything once familiar becomes unfamiliar. The emotional pain is inconceivable to those who've not suffered the death of their child. This is in part why most newly-bereaved parents do not believe they will survive. I'll talk about how I've taken life one day at a time for several years while learning to adapt to a world in which my daughter and wife no longer physically exist."

Patty's eyes teared up as she watched Rick's expression change. His brows became furrowed and his eyes glassed over when he was talking about the murders of his wife and daughter. "Telling your story will no doubt help several others, Rick. I'm proud of you for being willing to talk about your loss to a group who very much need to hear from someone who can explain that the process of adapting is something that continues during the rest of one's life, and that during these years you can find purpose and happiness again."

"Thanks, Patty. It's not an easy topic to discuss, but I'll feel good about using my loss toward helping others, if I can."

"You will," Patty said. The detectives each began reviewing the files on their desks when Patty's cell phone rang, and she saw again that it was her daughter. "It's Bec. Maybe she'll have an update on Mom and Bill."

Rick nodded with interest.

"Hey, Bec."

"Hi, Mom. I was able to talk with Grandma. She and Bill sure enjoyed last weekend. She said it was extra special since they'll be home for the next three months. They're at the hospital now, and I've promised to bring over the first casserole when they get back."

"That's great, Bec," Patty said. "I'm sure your call lifted her spirits."

"She said it did, Mom. As a matter of fact, she asked me a philosophical question and asked that I pass both the question and answer on to you."

Patty looked at Rick and rolled her eyes. "I'm putting you on speakerphone, Bec, so that Rick can get in on this. Want to repeat what you just said?"

Rick called out, "Hi, Becky."

"Hey, Rick. So, you know how my grandma periodically presents a philosophical question to us all?"

"I do," said Rick, already chuckling as he thought of some of Maggie's past questions.

Becky laughed in response to Rick, and Patty smiled, waiting for the question.

"So," Becky said, "do you know why the weather on our planet is constantly vacillating back and forth between angry, severe weather days, such as we experience in the winter, and sunny, calm, serene days such as we have in summer?"

"Uh," Rick started, "because of the tides?"

"Nope," Becky said. "You have a guess, Mom?"

"Because of collisions of heavenly bodies going on within the universe?"

"No again," Becky said. "Any other guesses?"

Rick and Patty looked at each other and shook their heads. "We've got nothing," Patty said. "What is your grandma's answer?"

Becky started laughing again. "It's because the Earth is bi-polar!"

Rick chuckled as Becky continued laughing at her end of the line. Patty who could usually keep a straight face at her mother's questions couldn't do so this time.

"Well," Patty said, "seems Maggie O'Toole hasn't lost her sense of humor."

"I've got to get back to my homework," Becky said. "Grandma told me you two are looking for a killer. Hope you catch whoever it is."

"Thanks, Bec," Patty said. "And thanks for passing on your grandma's question. I think that's one of the better ones. See you tonight."

"Bye, Becky," Rick said.

"See ya, Rick."

Still smiling from the joke, Patty looked up to see Brad walk in. "I've got the files you requested from former Detective Rogers. There's one on Sorenson and one on Faires."

Patty's cell phone jingled for an incoming text. "This is Pete," she said. "Baird has just returned home."

Brad placed the files on Patty's desk. "I'll meet you out there and wait for instruction."

Rick stood up and felt for his gun. "I'll drive," he said.

Patty stood, preparing to leave. It took about eight minutes for the detectives to arrive in front of Baird's home. Brad had arrived before them. Patty picked up the radio microphone, thumbed the button, and spoke to Brad. "Go ahead and walk around to the back and wait there until I let you know that we're in. Ask Pete to cover the front once we're inside. We don't want this guy to run."

"Copy that," Brad said.

The detectives waited in the car until Brad left his and walked around to the back. Pete pulled his car up so that he was directly in front of the suspect's house.

Rick knocked on the front door. After waiting a few minutes, he was about to knock again when the door slowly opened. Patty and Rick showed their badges, and Patty introduced them. "We're Detectives O'Toole and Starker. We'd like to talk with you for a few minutes about your neighbor. May we come in?"

Baird looked at Patty as she spoke and then at Rick. "No," he said. "I spoke with a couple of cops this morning and I've got nothing more to say."

Patty glanced at Rick who then took a couple of steps backward and turned to the side so as to appear less threatening, leaving Patty to talk with Baird. "I'm sorry to bother you again, Mr. Baird. The officers here this morning forgot to ask a couple of questions. We'll only need a few minutes of your time and you'd really be helping us out, sir."

Baird stared at Patty, shook his head back and forth, and then stared again at her as he let out a sigh, but said nothing.

Patty furrowed her brow a bit and addressed him again. "Please, Mr. Baird, our lieutenant told us to ask you these questions, and we promise it'll only take a couple minutes of your time. We'd hate for the lieutenant to send us back here. We really don't want to bother you a third time."

"Oh, okay," he said, opening the door. "If it's just two questions and then you'll leave."

Patty and Rick walked through the front door into the living room. "Thank you, Mr. Baird," Patty said as she opened her notepad. "We appreciate your giving us your time."

Rick walked over to the couch to sit down, and Baird quickly protested, "You don't need to sit down. You said you'd only be here for a few minutes."

Rick sat down and jumped back up before Baird could finish. "Ow," Rick said. "What was that?"

Rick, Baird and Patty all stared at the barrel of a handgun sticking out where the seat and back cushions came together.

"Well, what have we here?" Rick asked.

Patty responded before Baird could answer. "Hands behind your head," she said.

"That isn't mine!" Baird yelled out. "I don't know how it got there," he yelled as he backed up to the wall.

Patty took her handcuffs out and, taking hold of Baird, turned one of his arms at a time down and behind his back as she cuffed him. Rick called Pete on his portable radio. "There's a camera in the console of my car and evidence bags in the trunk. Bring in the camera and an evidence bag."

"Copy that," Pete said.

Rick then let Brad know that they had Baird in cuffs.

Baird called out again. "Someone else left it there. Must have been when I had a few friends over a couple nights ago."

"We're taking you down to the station," Patty said. "We'll call your PO and you can tell her how the gun got there."

Pete walked in and handed the camera to Rick, who had put a CS glove on his right hand. He took several photos and then placed the gun in the evidence bag, pulled a black pen from his pocket, and signed and dated the evidence chain form printed on the bag. He gave the bag to Pete. "Take this to the station and lock it up in evidence."

Brad walked into the room. "You need anything more from me?"

"Let's step out on the porch," Rick said to him.

Brad followed Rick out to the front porch and down the steps where they could talk without being heard. "We found a handgun on his couch. Pete will put it into evidence. You take Baird to the holding cell."

Brad nodded. "Will do," he said as he started back up the steps.

"Did you and Pete have a chance to finish your canvassing?" Rick asked.

Brad stopped and turned around. "We did. There's one other neighbor, in addition to the elderly one, who noticed the blue car with one working taillight. I'll put the name and address on your desk."

"Great," Rick said.

Patty and Rick locked the house and started back to their office. Rick chuckled. "You have a way with the gentlemen, Detective O'Toole. That went quite well."

Patty smiled. "Oh? Well, I don't know about having a way with anyone, but I'm glad we found cause for our search warrant. We may have run out of time if you hadn't found that gun so quickly. I'll request the warrant as soon as we get back and hope to have it in our hands tomorrow. Right now, I need to make a call to Baird's PO." Patty tapped in the Josephine County number on her cell phone. Two rings later the phone was answered.

"Wakely."

"PO Wakely, this is Detective O'Toole. We were able to enter the house and we've arrested Baird for being a felon in possession of a firearm. We'll use this to get our search warrant."

"Doesn't surprise me," Wakely said. "Now I highly suspect we'll find stolen property in his house and the gun may be part of it. Let me know when your warrant comes through. Can you keep Baird in lockup there until we search his house?"

"Shouldn't be a problem. I'm guessing we'll have the warrant within a few hours after my request. If there's no evidence of a crime here in Brookings, we'll need to hand him over to you."

"There's room for him here. The firearm will send him back and probably get him another couple of years."

"We'll be in touch," Patty said. After ending the call Patty got to work writing the search warrant affidavit while Rick wrote the report on finding the gun. When she was finished, Patty picked up the files Brad had brought in.

"I'll look at Sorenson's file," Patty said, "if you want to start with Faires'."

Rick reached across his desk and took the file from Patty. "Shouldn't take long," he said, "if this is all they had for him."

"Both files are pretty thin," Patty said. "Another indication of a small department."

Several minutes later Rick closed the file. "No background," he said.

"Nothing?" Patty asked.

Rick shook his head. "Seems Faires was hired based solely on his application."

"What were his jobs prior to being hired on in Arcadia?"

"He was a police officer for two years in a small Arkansas town called Prairie Grove and then worked as a security guard for a couple months before Arcadia hired him."

"Does he say why he left the Prairie Grove job?"

"He wrote on his application that he left due to boredom. Wanted to be more active."

"Well," said Patty, "that could be the case, but we need to talk with the agency and find out if that's the real reason he left. Is there a contact name or number in there?"

"There's a name. Chief Walker. No number."

Patty googled the police department. "Here it is," she said. "Let me make a call now and find out if there was some other reason our suspect left his job after only two years."

CHAPTER 11

An automated answering service provided the greeting when Patty called the number she found. "This is your Prairie Grove Police Department. We're open from eight A.M. to five P.M. seven days a week. You are either calling at a time when we're closed, or the receptionist is away from her desk. At the sound of the tone, please leave your name, phone number, and a brief message. We'll get back with you as soon as we can. Y'all have a nice day and thank you for calling your Prairie Grove Police Department."

Patty waited for the beep and then left a message. "This is Detective O'Toole with the Brookings, Oregon police department. I'd like to talk with Chief Walker." She left her phone numbers and hung up. "Well, they are certainly a friendly agency there in Prairie Grove."

Before the detectives could continue their conversation, Patty's cell phone rang. She glanced at caller ID. "This is Prairie Grove PD," she said to Rick before answering the call. "Detective O'Toole," she stated into the receiver.

A woman with a quiet, squeaky voice spoke to Patty. "Oh, Detective, this is Mary Lu from the Prairie Grove Police Department. I'm sorry I didn't answer your call just now. I left my desk for just a minute and didn't make it back before our voicemail greeting turned on."

"No problem," said Patty. "Is your chief there?"

"He is, Detective. Please hold on while I transfer you."

"Detective O'Toole, this is Chief Walker. What can I do for you?"

"Thank you, Chief. I'm going to put you on speakerphone so that my partner, Detective Starker, can participate in the call." Patty touched the speaker button and continued to talk. "We've had a murder here in Brookings and we're investigating a couple of people, one of whom is Morten Faires. In reviewing Mr. Faires' personnel file from Arcadia, Louisiana, we've read that he worked two years for your agency prior to being hired on by Arcadia. Do you remember Mr. Faires?"

"Oh, I remember him alright. Hiring him was the worse decision I've ever made for my department and one I regret to this day. What's he done to make him a suspect in your murder case?"

"At this time we're not calling him a suspect. He's more a person of interest. The information in his file tells us that Prairie Grove PD put Faires through the academy. Is this correct?"

"We did," said the chief. "As I recall, he had relatives that were both military and law enforcement, and we figured that was background enough for us. We were also in great need of another officer. Nothing during his verbal interview suggested to us that he wasn't going to be good for the department."

"Well," said Patty, "your responses to our questions might be of great help to our investigation."

"Go ahead and ask your questions," said the chief.

"Our first question is why Faires left your department. Did he leave for another job or was he terminated?"

"He was terminated, and none too soon."

"Can you tell us about the reason for his termination?" Patty asked.

"Sure, but I'll start before the termination. He was in trouble and written up within four months of working patrol."

"What was the problem?" Patty asked.

"A citizen filed a complaint against him. Said that Faires stopped him for a traffic violation, and when the citizen expressed that Faires was wrong, Faires became verbally abusive. A second event happened three weeks later. Again, Faires stopped a citizen for speeding. The citizen expressed in court that he wasn't speeding, and when he spoke up to the officer, Faires put his hand around the butt of his gun and told the citizen that he'd better just accept the ticket if he knew what was good for him."

"Is that when you terminated him?" Patty asked.

"Unfortunately not," said the chief. "We're a small agency, and for years we've had a difficult time attracting employees and even a harder time keeping them with us. We were certain when Faires applied that he was what we needed. That's why we spent the money to put him through the academy."

Rick asked the next question. "What made you so sure that Faires would be a good cop when he'd had no formal training?"

"Family history," said the chief. "Faires' dad and uncle each served twenty years in the military, and he has a cousin who's a police officer in Natchez, Louisiana."

Patty raised her eyebrows. "You figured you were hiring a well-disciplined guy who would perform well."

"That's exactly what we thought," said the chief.

"So," Patty asked, "what did he do that resulted in his termination?"

"The incident that got him terminated," said the chief, "was a complaint by a teenage girl. She claimed that Faires stopped her and said that she was speeding. When the girl protested, Faires offered to drop the charge if she'd take a ride with him in his patrol car. The girl refused and Faires wrote her up."

Rick interrupted. "That sounds like another 'he said, she said' incident. How is it that this one got him fired?"

"Well," said the chief, "the young girl is the niece of Judge Wilson who was the presiding judge on the day Faires and the girl went to court. The judge knew his niece pretty well and decided in her favor."

"How," Patty asked, "did Faires respond to the judge?"

"He had no response," said the chief, "at least not in the courtroom. He simply stood up and walked out. When he left the building, I followed in time to see him get into his patrol car, turn on the lights and siren, and speed off."

"I take it he wasn't responding to a call," Patty said.

"No call," said the chief. "The next day I called him into my office and terminated him."

"I think you made the right decision, Chief," Rick said.

The chief laughed. "I think it was the only right decision I made about Faires. He was surprisingly a huge disappointment."

"Thanks, Chief," Patty said. "That's all I have. You have any more questions, Rick?"

"I do. Chief, do you remember how the young girl described in court what Faires was like when he stopped her?"

"I sure do. She said he was creepy and put his hand on her arm when he suggested she get into his car. She said that his expression darkened considerably when she refused. He wrote up the ticket, threw it into the car, and then said he'd be watching her. She repeated the term 'creepy' a few times as she described the incident."

The detectives both noted the description. "Thanks, Chief," Rick said.

"Before you go," the chief said, "I've got a question for you. You said he left us and went to work for Arcadia PD. Did they terminate him too?"

"They did," Patty said.

"What for?" the chief asked.

"You'll need to talk with Arcadia Police Chief Todd for that information," Patty said. "Thank you again for your assistance."

"No problem," the chief said. "I hope that whatever you find on Faires, it's enough to keep him from working again in law enforcement. We don't need guys like him in our line of work."

"We understand," Patty said. "Thanks again for your time."

After ending the call Rick shook his head. "Too bad Arcadia didn't do a background on Faires before hiring. I'm guessing they would have passed on him."

"I agree, Rick, but as of a few years ago I know that there were agencies here in Oregon that didn't do pre-employment backgrounds. I'll bet there are several that still don't do a background or, if they do, don't do what is considered a thorough one."

"Why do you think that is?" Rick asked.

Patty shrugged her shoulders. "They're expensive if you have a lot of turnover, and small agencies may not have anyone in-house with the training to do a proper one."

Rick shook his head. "I'm betting Chief Todd might begin doing them once he's told what we now know about Faires. Learning about the Prairie Grove incidents before hiring Faires might have saved Arcadia a lot of frustration."

"Not to mention a couple of lives, if Faires is our guy," Patty said.

"Before we begin on the Sorenson file," Rick said, "I'm wondering if you noticed the weather report for tomorrow. We're supposed to have thirty-five-foot waves! I read about them last year and probably the year before, but I've not had the time to watch."

"I did see that report," Patty said. "We should plan on using part of our lunch hour down at the harbor beach where a lot of people go to see the drama. Those high waves are pretty impressive."

"I'll bet," Rick said. "It's interesting that the high waves don't necessarily correlate to a big storm."

"They're actually more fun to watch," Patty said, "when we don't have heavy rain being blown about. Easier to see. The effect of those high waves crashing up against a one-hundred-foot-high sea stack is pretty spectacular. Like water fireworks!"

"Wow!" said Rick. "I need to see that. I wrote to a Boston buddy just the other day about our sea stacks. I explained to him what you told me about our prehistoric rocks. It's great to be able to look out on something created millions of years ago and formed by nature."

Patty smiled. "What was his response?"

"He wants to come visit and probably will make it out here next month."

"I'm guessing he'll be impressed," Patty said, "even if we don't have thirty-five-foot waves while he's visiting. I've heard from many world travelers that we have one of the most beautiful coastlines across the globe."

Rick nodded. "Well, my friend hasn't been around the world, but he's seen the New England Atlantic coast and I'm guessing he'll find our coastline at least as impressive. I wonder what I need to do for him to see a whale while he's out here."

Patty laughed. "Now you're asking for too much. Spotting whales is a hit-and-miss thing. You just have to get lucky."

"Maybe so," said Rick.

Patty opened the file on her desk. "So, let's see if there are contact numbers in Sorenson's file for any relatives he may have. In addition to letting relatives know what's happened, it would be good to know if Sorenson had anything of value before we search Baird's house. I'll take care of this if you'll call Chief Todd and get names and contact information for officers who worked with Sorenson."

"Will do," Rick said. "In addition to asking about Sorenson, I'll ask each what they thought of Faires. Maybe we'll find out more than we heard from the chief."

"Could be," Patty said as she picked up her cell phone and called the number for Sorenson's only relative mentioned in his personnel file.

After three rings a man answered the call. "Hello?"

"Hello, sir. This is Detective O'Toole with the Brookings, OR police department. Are you Joseph Sorenson?"

"I am. What's this call about?"

"Do you have a brother Jonas Sorenson?"

"I do," he said.

"Mr. Sorenson," Patty began, "I'm sorry to have to tell you this over the phone. Your brother is deceased."

Patty heard a quick intake of breath on the other end of the call. "Deceased? When?"

"He died last Thursday."

"How?"

"This will be difficult to hear, Mr. Sorenson. Your brother was murdered. He was hanged."

"Oh, no! I just spoke with him two weeks ago. I was planning a trip to Oregon next spring to see him. He was relaxed and happy for the first time in years. Do you know who did it?"

"We don't, but we have started a full investigation. I'd like to ask you a few questions. Is this a good time?"

"I guess so. This is just such a shock. He was my only sibling and the rest of our family is gone."

"If you need time by yourself, Mr. Sorenson, I can certainly call back later."

"No. You need to catch whoever did this. Go ahead and ask your questions."

"Okay," said Patty. "Do you know anyone who held a grudge against your brother or may have wanted to hurt him?"

"You probably know, Detective, that my brother was a cop. He was a good cop and took his job of protecting the public seriously. He helped put a lot of bad guys in jail and for this reason I'm sure there are many people who didn't like him. I didn't know the officers he worked with because he lived in Louisiana when he was in law enforcement, and I've lived the past twenty years in Idaho. His move to Brookings was in part to shorten the distance between our two homes so that we could see each other at least once a year."

Patty made notes as Joseph Sorenson spoke. "Do you remember any childhood friends he didn't get along with?"

"No. The kids in our neighborhood all liked Jonas. He had a great sense of humor, and even as a kid he had a lot of compassion for those who couldn't defend themselves. Between his humor and compassion he got along with everyone. He served four years in the Marine Corps before going into law enforcement, and I can remember an event where several of Jonas' Marine Corps buddies told stories about how his humor got them all through boot camp. He made sergeant within those four years and I'm sure his personality helped."

"Thanks, Mr. Sorenson. Now I'd like to ask about your brother's assets. Do you know if he had anything of value in his home?"

"I was only in his home once and that was in January of this year. I don't recall any furnishings that were noticeably valuable, but Jonas did show me his coin collection.

"He started collecting coins when we were kids and, much to my surprise, had continued building his collection over the years. He told me what it was worth because he said I was his beneficiary and he didn't want me thinking it was of little value and giving it to a second-hand store or something if he predeceased me."

There was a long pause before Patty asked, "You okay to go on?"

"Sure. It's just really sad. Neither of us intended for me to be inheriting his coins for at least another twenty years or so. I just can't believe he's gone."

"I understand, Mr. Sorenson. Do you remember what Jonas said the coins were worth?"

"Seven thousand dollars. He'd had them appraised just a few months before I made that trip."

"Did he happen to tell you where in his home he kept them?"

"When I was there, he kept them in a box on one of his living room bookshelves."

"Like a shoe box?" Rick asked.

"Bigger. And it had the American flag painted on the lid. Why are you asking me about the coins? Are they no longer there?"

Patty softened her voice. "I'm afraid not."

"Oh, no. I hope he wasn't murdered for the coin collection."

"We don't yet know why he was murdered," Patty said. "But we want to gather as much information as we can so as to expand our search to cover any reason someone may have had to commit the crime."

Sorenson interrupted Patty. "There is one thing, Detective, I don't know if this is important, but I just remembered that Jonas told me there was a girl he'd started to date. Someone he'd recently met."

"Do you remember," asked Patty, "if he gave you her name or mentioned where she worked?"

"Yeah, her name is Pearl. I don't remember Jonas mentioning her last name. He said she waited tables at that casino just south of Brookings."

"He give you any other information such as how often he saw her or whether she was moving in with him?"

"No," said Sorenson. "He didn't say much except that during my visit we'd eat at the casino on a day she was working so I could meet her. I got the impression he'd only met her recently and that they hadn't dated much."

"Okay," Patty said. "That's all the questions I have right now. I need to give you the name of the funeral home here in Brookings where your brother was taken. Before I do, are there any questions you'd like to ask me?"

"Will you let me know if you catch the person who did this?"

"We will," Patty said.

"I guess," said Sorenson, "that I need to find an attorney. Jonas gave me a copy of his trust. The original is in a safe deposit box there in Brookings."

"That would be a good idea," said Patty. "Do you have a pen and paper so that I can give you the funeral home's contact information?"

"Give me a minute."

Patty waited and could hear the steps become quieter and then louder again as Sorenson walked away and then back to the phone. "Go ahead."

Patty gave him the information he needed for the funeral home and both of her phone numbers. "Please feel free to contact me anytime you have questions, and certainly if you'd like to meet my partner and me while you're in Brookings."

"I'll think about that," he said.

"Thank you for your time, Mr. Sorenson, and again, I'm so sorry for your loss."

"Sure, Detective. Thanks for letting me know. I'll call when I get out there."

Patty ended the call and looked up at Rick, who was making notes in the file on his desk. Hearing Patty end the call he looked up and saw her slump her shoulders and lower her head.

"That was hard," she said.

"Yeah, I could tell, listening to your side of the conversation. From what I could hear, seems our victim did have something of value."

"He did," Patty said. "A coin collection worth seven thousand dollars."

Rick gave out a low whistle. "A collection that valuable could probably be fenced in Smith River for about two thousand, and there's a lot of people between Crescent City and Brookings who'd have no problem breaking into a home for that kind of money."

"Hummm," Patty said. "Mr. Baird seems to be one such person. I think there's a good chance we'll find the coins at his place if he hasn't already got rid of them. I was hoping the judge would have approved our search warrant today but given it's about five, it seems we may have to wait until morning. You have any luck calling Chief Todd?"

"I had to leave a message. I agree that we call it a day and start again tomorrow."

Chapter 12

Both detectives stood up to leave as Brad quickly walked into the room waving the search warrant. "Got it!" he said, handing it to Patty. She thanked Brad and looked at Rick, who had already put his jacket on.

"Guess there's no time like the present," he said. "Want me to drive?"

"Yep," she said. "I'll call PO Wakely and let her know we have the warrant. Given the hour, she may want to wait until tomorrow, but I'd like to know tonight if Sorenson's coin collection is in that house."

The detectives left the station and drove back to Baird's house. They performed the required ritual of knock-and-announce, and then using the key Baird had on him, they entered through the front door and put on their gloves and booties. "I'll start in the back," Patty said, "and work my way forward if you want to start in here."

"Maybe I'll search the couch first," Rick said, walking across the room. "I may find a coin collection under a cushion I didn't sit down on earlier."

Patty walked down the hall and started with the bathroom, checking under the toilet tank lid, in the cupboards, and the medicine cabinet. She then turned the doorknob on the bedroom closest to the bath and found the room was locked. "Hey, Rick."

"Yeah?"

"I need your help here."

Rick walked down the hall to where Patty was standing. "What's up? You find something?"

"No, I need you to open this door," Patty said with a smile.

"Is that all?" he said, stepping back. Rick kicked the door at the doorknob, busting it wide open. Both detectives stood quietly for a moment scanning the room.

"Looks like we hit the jackpot," Patty said.

"Yeah," said Rick. "PO Wakely's going to make a lot of Josephine County residents happy once the trial is over."

"If it does all belong to Josephine County," Patty said. "Let's get Brad and Pete back here to help us. You search the rest of the house while I begin listing everything on the receipt. We don't want to miss another room like this one. Brad and Pete can transport it all back to the department and log it in as evidence. The courthouse is closed so tomorrow morning I'll take the search warrant back to the judge with a copy of the receipt."

"I'll say this for Mr. Baird," Rick said. "He must be a guy who plans his year. Looks like he was saving up for the winter when residents tend to be home, making it more difficult to find homes to burglarize."

"I guess," Patty said, shaking her head.

Five minutes later Rick returned to the room where Patty was finishing up the receipt. "Nothing in the rest of the house so he must have stashed it all in this room. You find the coin collection?"

"No," Patty said. "But I do recognize some jewelry that was reported stolen a couple weeks ago. The owners were smart and had photographs to give us."

"Brad and Pete should be here soon," Rick said. "I'll take a few photographs while we wait."

When Brad and Pete arrived, Rick and Patty left a copy of the completed receipt in the house and started back to their office.

"Glad our search warrant had results," Rick said.

"The judge will be happy," Patty said with a smile. "I think he rushed it for us."

* * *

Patty arrived early the next day and found Rick at his desk on the phone. She took her coffee cup into the break room and returned to her desk with it full, along with doughnuts for herself and Rick. He gave her the thumbs-up sign when he saw what she set on his desk. She took off her jacket and headed back out of the office and down the hall to brief the lieutenant.

"Good morning, O'Toole," he greeted her.

"Good morning, LT. Got time for an update?"

"I do," he said.

"We spoke with Joseph Sorenson, brother to Jonas Sorenson. Our victim retired five years ago and two years later bought his house here. Joseph, who lives in Idaho, said that he and Jonas were fairly close. It was Joseph who told us about his brother's seven thousand-dollar coin collection. He also told me about a casino waitress who Jonas had recently started seeing."

"Have you contacted her?" asked the lieutenant.

"We plan to do that later today," Patty said.

"Has the state lab come back with anything yet?"

"We're still waiting," said Patty. "I can also give you an update on Baird, the neighbor of Sorenson. As you read in Rick's written report, we found a gun when Baird allowed us into his house and then requested a search warrant based upon a felon in possession of a firearm. We didn't find Sorenson's coin collection, but we did find a room full of various items, all of which, we assume, are stolen goods. I recognized a couple pieces of jewelry from a burglary here, but we figure the bulk of it is out of Josephine County."

"That's good," the lieutenant said without changing his expression. "Have you let PO Wakely know?"

"I left her a message on my way home last night. I expect she'll be eager to get over here with one of their deputies and get photos and descriptions of the property. There appeared to be enough to close more than a few cases. I just wish we'd found the coins. It would have felt good to tell Sorenson's brother while he's out here."

"Don't give up on it yet. Baird may talk once he learns how much more time he'll do for both the illegal possession of a firearm and the thefts. If he fenced the coins before you searched the house, he may give up where. Do you see him as a possible suspect for the murder?"

"We haven't ruled him out," said Patty. "Whoever committed the murder was pretty savvy about leaving evidence. We'll have a better idea about Baird's capabilities after we talk with him."

"Well, keep on it," said the lieutenant. "You learn anything else about Faires?"

"We have. We've reviewed his employment file at Arcadia, and they didn't do a background. We also discovered that, prior to Arcadia, Faires worked a couple of years at a small agency in Prairie Grove, Arkansas, where they put him through the academy."

"That," said the lieutenant, "would have given him organizational and investigation skills, and provided knowledge of law enforcement's use of restraints. Anything else?"

"Not now."

"Thanks for the update," said the lieutenant. "You and Rick keep investigating and you'll find our responsible."

"Thanks, LT. I'll keep you posted."

Patty returned to the office and before she could sit down, heard the radio crackle. 911 had received a silent alarm from the local bank. Brad immediately responded, telling Dispatch to have the manager step outside to meet him. Rick put the second half of his doughnut back down on a napkin, stood, and checked his gun. Patty put her jacket back on and let the dispatcher know that she and Rick were on their way. Before they'd driven the five blocks to the bank, they heard Brad's voice on the radio. "I think I see him. There's a guy on a bike riding west on Fern Avenue, WMA, forties, medium build, blue jeans, and a black and red shirt."

Patty and Rick looked at each other, then Patty spoke into the microphone. "What makes you think the guy on the motorcycle is the bank robber?"

"Not a motorcycle," Brad said. "A bicycle, and he must have just hit a pothole because he's been thrown off the bike. I'll be out on foot."

As the detectives pulled into the bank, the radio crackled again, and Pete let Dispatch know that he was on the scene with Brad and they had their suspect in custody.

Patty used her cell phone to call Pete, who picked up on the first ring, seeing it was the detective. "We've got him, Detective."

"Are you sure it's him?" Patty asked.

"Well, he's got a Fred Meyer grocery bag full of money."

"How do you know it's money stolen from the bank?" Patty asked.

"I know because the bank gave him the dye pack. There's red dye all over the money, the suspect's hands, and his shirt."

Patty laughed. "Good work, officers," she said to Brad as she walked over to Rick, who was talking with the branch manager.

Rick smiled. "They gave him the dye pack."

"Pete told me," Patty said.

The branch manager smiled. "And it worked beautifully."

When the detectives finished up at the bank, Rick reminded Patty that it was almost lunch time. On the way out of town Rick commented, "After this bank robbery you can't complain about not having any stories to tell like I do about Boston. A bank robber with a bike as a getaway vehicle is funny enough. But to also be given the dye pack makes it hilarious."

"I guess you're right," Patty laughed. "I do have a few stories to tell."

Rick drove the twelve miles to the Lucky Seven Casino, passing a herd of elk on the way. "I'm always a little surprised at how many people stop on the narrow shoulder of this highway to watch the elk. Seems they're not concerned at all about being rear-ended."

"I think that seeing an elk up that close is pretty rare for people coming from other areas of the country," Patty said. "I agree that it's dangerous, but not everyone thinks about the danger. They just want a cool photo to take home, and elk are beautiful animals."

Rick pulled into the casino parking lot. "The lot's pretty full for this time of day. I wonder how many of them are hoping to take home that?" he asked, looking toward the shiny new car on top of a platform that had been hydraulically lifted about ten feet into the air.

"There's probably a steady stream of people stopping in who see the billboard beckoning them to take a chance. Sadly, many will spend money they can't afford to lose. Not everyone who comes here is a gambler, though. I know several people who enjoy the food."

Rick opened the restaurant door for Patty. "Let's hope we find Pearl serving some of that fine food now."

Walking into the restaurant, Patty was approached by a woman with an armful of menus. "Lunch for two?"

"No, thank you," Patty said, showing her badge. "We're here to talk with one of your servers. Is Pearl here today?"

The woman turned and pointed to a waitress delivering food to a table of four. "That's Pearl."

"Would you let her know we'd like to talk with her?" Patty asked.

The woman walked over to Pearl as she finished at the table. Pearl looked up at the detectives and walked over. "I'm Pearl."

"We're Detectives O'Toole and Starker," Patty said. "We'd like to ask you a few questions. Is there someplace where we can talk?"

"We can sit at the empty table there in the corner since it's not too busy right now," she said, leading the detectives across the room. "Is this about Jonas?" she asked Patty after sitting down.

"Why do you ask if we're here about Jonas?"

"Well, because I've done nothing to give you a reason to need to talk with me. I figure someone told you that Jonas and I dated a few times, and now that he's dead, you want to know more about me."

"Where were you last Wednesday, the night before Jonas was found?" Patty asked.

"I was working here, and my boss will confirm that."

"Where did you go after work?"

Pearl looked at the table and turned her head, looking out the window. "I spent the night with a friend."

Rick was making notes in his small pocket tablet. "The name of your friend?" he asked.

"Why are you asking me these questions? You don't think I could have killed Jonas, do you?"

"We don't know who killed Mr. Sorenson," Patty said, "but it's our job to find out, and that requires talking with everyone who knew him. This is a murder investigation."

Rick repeated his earlier question. "What is the name of your friend, and a contact number?"

"Look," Pearl said. "He's married and I don't want to get him in trouble. Will you make sure his wife doesn't know what you're talking about if you have to call him?"

"We'll only talk with him if we need to," Rick said.

"Okay. His name is Harold, Harold Bochner, and you can reach him at the number for the casino."

"When is the last time you saw Jonas?" Patty asked.

"Last week. He met me here at the end of my shift."

"What day last week?" Rick asked.

"Tuesday."

Rick looked down at his notes. "So you saw Jonas on Tuesday and spent the night with Harold the next day?"

"It isn't what you think," Pearl said. "Harold and I have known each other for three years. I only met Jonas a few months ago, and for a long time we just spoke when he'd come to eat. We really didn't start dating until a few weeks ago. I mean I like him and all, but I didn't know yet how serious we were going to be."

Rick nodded. "And you didn't want to give up Harold if things didn't work out with you and Jonas."

Pearl shrugged. "I've learned to look out for myself."

"We understand, Pearl," Patty said. "Tell me, do you recall anything of value in Jonas's house? Anything that someone might want to break in and steal?"

Pearl sat quietly for a moment, shifting uncomfortably as she stared out the window. "No," she said. "I was only at his place a couple times and really didn't notice what he had in his house." She turned to check on her tables. "I need to get back to work," she said.

"Okay, Pearl," Patty said. "Thank you. Here's my card if you think of anything more about Mr. Sorenson."

"Before we go," Rick said, "let's take a look inside and find out if Harold is working today."

"It would be good to know if he's capable of lifting Sorenson," Patty said as they walked from the restaurant into the casino area. "We can ask at the cash window."

At the window Rick showed his badge. "Is Harold Bochner here today?"

"Just a minute," said the woman at the window as she picked up a phone receiver and tapped two of the buttons. "A couple detectives are here to see you," she said.

A few minutes later Harold walked up to the window. "What can I help you with?" he asked.

Patty responded, "We're investigating the murder of Jonas Sorenson and asking questions of anyone who knew him."

"I read about that in the paper, but I didn't know him."

"Do you remember seeing him here in the casino or in the restaurant?" Patty asked.

Harold stared at Patty. "No," he said.

Patty stared back at Harold. "Where were you last Wednesday night, the night before Sorenson's body was found?"

Harold paused, looked at Rick and back at Patty. "I was with my girl-friend."

"And her name?" Rick asked.

"Pearl," he said.

"Her last name?" Rick asked.

"No last name. Just Pearl. I've got work to do here, Detectives."

"We'll let you know if we need to talk again with you," Patty said. "Here's my card. Please call if you remember anything relating to Jonas Sorenson."

Patty and Rick left the casino and walked to their car. "He's as big as you are, Rick," Patty said.

"He is," said Rick. "I don't think he'd have any problem picking up our victim and hanging him from a tree."

"He's got motive, too," Patty said. "He might be a little obsessive about Pearl and thought Jonas was coming between them."

"Could be," Rick said, "and after talking to Pearl, I'm thinking Jonas knew nothing about Harold Bochner."

Patty agreed. "I get the same impression. Let's head back to the office."

Time is passing and you're no closer to catching me now than you were the day you cut down my victim. To tell the truth, Detectives, it's all starting to bore me and I'm beginning to feel hungry again. There's a loose end I need to tie up.

Chapter 13

As Rick drove back, Patty's cell phone rang. She looked at caller ID and saw it was her mom. "Detective O'Toole," she announced.

"Hello, Detective O'Toole, this is your mother."

Patty smiled. "Hi, Mom. How's Bill doing after his surgery?"

"He's pretty sore, but that's to be expected. The doctor said it could be three months before he's completely out of pain and has his energy back. He's pretty tired and I've encouraged him to sleep as much as he can so that his body can heal."

"That's good, Mom. I'm glad he has you. Can I bring over some dinner when you get home tomorrow?"

"Thanks, dear, but we're fine. Becky will drop off a casserole and that should take care of us for a few days. There is something I want to ask about, though, completely unrelated to Bill and me."

"Sure, Mom. What is it?"

"I have a friend at the senior center whose husband died recently. She is concerned about protecting herself and wants to be able to use a gun if necessary. He left her a 1911 handgun. My friend would like to use it, but she isn't strong enough. Somewhere in the back of my mind I remember you mentioning a gun part that can be purchased for the 1911 to make it easier to rack the slide. Do you know what I'm talking about?"

"I do, Mom. The 1911 gun part is a special hammer and it's called the Cammer. Having the Cammer installed in the 1911 reduces by about thirty-one percent the amount of strength necessary to rack the slide."

"That's it. I told my friend that you've given firearms training to groups of women and that you recommend the Cammer."

"I have. It's a great gift to the 1911 industry, not just for women but for people with arthritis in their hands, or those whose jobs, like law enforcement or the military, put them in situations when their hands might be wet or bloody."

"That's exactly what she needs, Patty. Can you give me their website address or a phone number so that I can pass it on to her?'

"It's Cammertechnologies.com and their phone number is on the front page of the site. Let her know to call me if she wants to talk with me about it."

"Thanks, Patty. I'll do that. She's had her concealed handgun license for years, but I've encouraged her to take a firearms course again, once the Cammer is in her gun. I'm sure she'll sleep better knowing she can defend herself if she's ever challenged."

"You've given her good advice, Mom. Rick and I just pulled up to the station. Was there anything else you needed to discuss?"

"Nothing I can think of now, dear. Tell Rick I said hi. Hope you catch the bad guys or gals."

"We're trying, Mom. Tell Bill we're thinking of him, and I'll talk with you later."

Patty hung up her cell phone. When she and Rick walked into the building and back to their desks, she saw that she had five messages on her landline. She connected with voicemail and began making notes on the small yellow pad she kept on her desk. After listening to the third message, she hung up and waited for Rick to be free. "I've got a voicemail message I want you to hear. It's an anonymous call from someone who says Pearl has a son we might want to look at for Jonas Sorenson's murder."

Patty played the call again as they both listened.

"The caller doesn't say how old Pearl's son is," said Rick, "but I have to assume he's over eighteen for you to get this call."

"And we may have another suspect," Patty said. "Let's talk again with Pearl and find out who her son is. I'll call the restaurant and see if she's working today." Patty tapped in the number from her file, asked about Pearl, and discovered that she still had a couple hours left in her shift. "I'd like to go out there now if you have time."

"I do," Rick said, standing up. "Seems Pearl may have a problem child."

At the casino restaurant the detectives could see that it was a lot busier than it had been when they'd spoken previously with Pearl. She came out of the kitchen with several plates in her hands and saw the detectives waiting up front. "You've caught me at a busy time of day," she said. "I get a break in ten minutes if you want to sit at a table and wait."

Patty looked at Rick and he nodded. The hostess then seated them at a table where they ordered and drank coffee for the ten-minute wait.

Patty watched Pearl as she crossed the room, sat down with the detectives, and started talking. "I told you all I know the last time you were here, and Harold said you talked to him. So why are you back?"

"Tell us about your son, Pearl," Patty said.

The skin color on Pearl's neck and face quickly turned a light red as she sat quietly, looking first at Patty and then at Rick.

"What's his name?" Rick asked.

"Why do you want to know about my son?"

"We told you before we're investigating a murder and questioning anyone who may have known Jonas Sorenson."

"My son didn't know Jonas."

"What's his name?" Patty asked.

Pearl looked around the room and then back at Patty. "I don't have to answer your questions, and I need to get back to work."

Patty leaned forward. "You can answer them for us now, or at the police station later. Your choice."

Pearl paused before responding. "His name is Kyle."

"And his last name?" Rick asked, writing in his pocket notebook.

"Rossmoor. Kyle Rossmoor."

"Thank you," said Patty. "We need to talk with Kyle, so we need a telephone number and his address."

"I can give you his number, but his phone doesn't always work. He lives behind the shopping center in Harbor."

Pearl gave Kyle's address to Rick and then looked again at Patty. "He didn't have anything to do with Jonas' death. He couldn't have."

"Why's that?" Patty asked.

"Because he wouldn't want to be locked up again."

Patty and Rick looked at each other and Rick asked, "Again?"

"Yeah. He has a problem with his temper."

"What was he put in jail for?" Patty asked.

"He was arrested once for road rage and another time for animal cruelty. A neighbor called the cops on him. I just can't believe that he'd do to an animal what the neighbor described. I think he was framed."

"Two more questions, Pearl," Patty said. "Did Kyle ever see Jonas' house? Maybe go there with you?"

"I was only at Jonas' house twice and Kyle didn't come in with me."

"He didn't go in with you? Does that mean that he was with you when you drove up but didn't go in?"

"I guess," Pearl said, "that he did drop me off the first time I was there. But he didn't go in."

"Last question," Patty said. "Did Jonas have anything of value in his house?"

Pearl's coloring seemed to change again. "I didn't see anything."

"Okay, Pearl," Patty said. "Thanks for your time. That's all the questions we have for now."

Patty and Rick returned to Rick's car and drove north to Brookings.

"Do you think she knows about the coin collection?" Patty asked.

"She certainly seemed to have a problem with the question so, yes, I think she does."

"We need to take a look at Kyle's arrest record," Patty said. "Based upon Pearl's description, he has tendencies that could easily result in murder if Kyle wanted those coins."

Rick nodded. "He certainly has a place on our suspect list. We'll know how close to the top of that list he is after we talk with him and read his record."

"When we get back to the office," Patty said, "let's go over again what we now have on the murder and list our key suspects."

"Sounds good to me," Rick said.

"So, changing the subject, you want to tell me more about salmon?" Patty asked.

"Sure. Salmon evolution is called 'anadromy' and it's an interesting subject. Salmon are born in fresh water, spend most of their lives at sea, and then return to fresh water to spawn. They may travel three thousand miles or more during the ocean leg of their migration."

"That's a lot," Patty said. "Why is there now so much debate over them?"

"The controversy about fish on the Columbia River isn't new. It's been going on since 1978 between the industrialists and the environmentalists. Both groups have the same goal: healthy salmon runs. They just can't agree on how to reach that goal. I'm guessing the differences of opinion will never end because there are now thousands of people who make a living from the ongoing disagreement. If they are not one of the attorneys, they either work for an attorney or for one of the organizations that hires attorneys to represent their point of view."

"And it's members of our society whose power comes from Bonneville Power Administration who pay for all of this?"

"About thirty percent of their bill," Rick said. "BPA markets the electric power generated by the Bonneville Dam located on the Columbia river.

"Who knew there'd be so much to learn about salmon?" Patty said as Rick pulled into the police station. "I'll take note of all that a salmon goes through in life when I take my next bite."

Rick laughed. "And think about the fact that you've paid twice for it. The first time was on your electric bill."

* * *

At her desk Patty pulled out a yellow pad. "Okay, let's go over what we've got from the beginning. You want to start?"

"Sure," Rick said, opening his file. "We've got one Jonas Sorenson who was hanged by Goldline rope in the rest stop across the highway from Harris Beach State Park. There were rope marks on the tree suggesting that the responsible practiced."

"Making this," Patty said, "a premeditated murder."

"The responsible used flex cuffs," Rick said.

Patty nodded. "Creating the possibility that he's had some law enforcement experience."

"There was a gash on the victim's head," Rick said, "suggesting that he was hit over the head prior to being hanged, and we don't yet have an ID on the weapon."

Patty continued down the list. "Cause of death was asphyxiation due to hanging, and we don't have a witness to the crime. What can we now add?"

"The victim owned a valuable coin collection," Rick said, "that was stolen from his home sometime within the past year and most likely prior to his death. We also know that shortly before he died, he began dating a local woman, Pearl, who claims not to have known about the coin collection."

"Pearl has a boyfriend, Harold Bochner, who works at the casino," Patty added. "Pearl was seeing him at the same time she started a relationship with our victim. Though Bochner said he didn't know our victim, he could have become jealous after discovering that Sorenson and Pearl had seen each other a couple of times. And then there's her son Kyle."

"Not just a son," Rick said, "but a son with a violent record who knows where the victim lived."

"The only relative of the victim we know of," said Patty, "is a brother, Joseph, who lives in Idaho."

Rick continued. "Baird, a man living across from the victim's house, has a record in Josephine County and is now in jail as a felon in possession of a firearm. He'll continue to do time for possession of stolen property we found in his house."

Patty looked up at Rick. "Let's make note of what we know about Faires thus far."

"He's a guy with seemingly psychopathic tendencies," Rick said, "who was terminated from two southern U.S. police departments, and whose whereabouts are now unknown."

"We know that our victim was one of two police sergeants responsible for Faires' termination from one of the two southern police departments, and that the second police sergeant responsible for Faires' termination was also found hanged. Thus far, we have no evidence as to who the responsible is on either of the two crimes."

The detectives paused for a minute looking over their list.

"So," Patty said, "who are our persons of interest?"

"Faires, definitely," Rick said. "He had a grudge against Sorenson."

Patty nodded. "Let's also list Baird. Could be he stole the coins and Sorenson found out and threatened to go to the police."

"Kyle Rossmoor is now on the list," Rick said. "A lot of sick adults started out torturing animals. Kyle must be in his thirties. For him to still be mistreating animals suggests that he has psychopathic tendencies."

"I agree, Rick. I'll take a look at Kyle's file before we approach him.

"I think we should also add Pearl and Harold to our list. It's clear that Pearl was not completely honest with us, and the two or three of them could have been working together. We need to know more about any association with Sorenson before we remove them from the list."

"While you review the file, I'm going to the break room for something to eat," Rick said. "My stomach is reminding me that we missed lunch. You want anything?"

"No, thanks. I've got some crackers I can eat while going over the file. When I'm done, I'll fill in the LT on where we are." Patty started reviewing the file on Kyle Rossmoor. At the time of his last arrest he was driving a navy blue four-door Ford Fiesta. She was interrupted by her cell phone and caller ID told her it was Joseph Sorenson. "Detective O'Toole," she answered.

"Detective, this is Joseph Sorenson. I'm flying out there tomorrow and wondered if you and Detective Starker would have time for a meeting."

"Of course," she said. "When do you expect to be in Brookings?"

"Well, my flight arrives in Crescent City at eight fifteen and I'll be renting a car at the airport. I could probably be at your office about nine forty-five or ten."

"Detective Starker isn't here right now, but that timing will work for me. I expect it will for him too. You have our address?"

"I have it," he said. "Would I be able to walk through my brother's house while I'm there?"

"I think we can arrange that," Patty said.

"Okay, I'll see you tomorrow about ten. I understand that flights into Crescent City can be delayed due to fog. I'll let you know if I'm going to be late."

"We're familiar with fog-caused flight delays. If that happens, just let us know. We'll work with it."

"Thanks, Detective. I'll see you tomorrow."

"You're welcome, Mr. Sorenson. Goodbye."

Patty ended the call and walked down the hall to talk with the lieutenant.

"Come in, O'Toole."

"Thanks, LT," Patty said, taking a seat. "Just want to give you an updated status on the homicide."

"What have you got?" asked the lieutenant.

"Rick and I spoke with the woman who dated Sorenson a couple of times. We met with her at the casino restaurant where her boyfriend also works. They alibi each other, saying they were together on the night before Sorenson was found. She claims to have only been in Sorenson's home a couple of times and denies knowing he had anything of value."

"You spoke with Sorenson's brother. Did he say anything about the relationship based upon what Jonas had told him?"

"He didn't have much," Patty said, "other than knowing his brother had met Pearl. Joseph is coming out here tomorrow and will meet with Rick and me. I'll ask him again."

"Did the woman mention whether Jonas knew she had a boyfriend?"

"According to her, Jonas didn't know. There is someone else in the picture now."

"Oh?" said the lieutenant.

"The woman has a thirty-three-year-old son with a criminal record. He's done time for road rage and animal cruelty. I've seen the file, LT, and it's hard to read about what he's done to animals."

After briefing the lieutenant, the detectives drove to the address for Kyle.

"Have you noticed," Patty said, "that it's already turning dark at five o'clock?"

"I have," Rick said. "It doesn't bother me, but I know a lot of people who have a hard time with the short days."

"I'm one of those people," Patty said. "I just have to focus on the long summer days and be thankful I don't live in Alaska, where they go for months with little sunlight."

They arrived at Kyle's address to find a two-story, six-unit apartment building with a yard full of weeds. Cardboard or plastic covered a window in each of two units. The detectives climbed the stairs to the second floor and knocked on the door.

"Not home," Rick said after knocking again. "Could be his mother called him when we left."

"Probably so," Patty said. "Let's put a BOLO out on him with instruction to notify us but not to stop him. He's got to come home some time."

The detectives walked down the staircase to the first story of apartments and toward their car. Once they were both seated, Rick turned to Patty. "I'd like to hold off on sending that BOLO. Let's move away from the front of the building and watch for a few minutes. Someone was looking out the window of the apartment directly under Kyle's and they ducked when we walked by."

"You think he's there and avoiding us?" Patty asked as Rick backed the car out of the driveway and onto the street. Five minutes later they heard a car door shut and saw a car pull out of the apartment building's driveway. "That looks like the car described in the file," Patty said. "It also fits the description Sorenson's neighbor gave for the small four-door that parked several times in front of her house."

"That's it," Rick said. "Right down to the taillight that's out."

Rick turned on his lights and siren and pulled up close behind Kyle, who then sped off. Patty called Dispatch. "This is Detectives O'Toole and Starker in pursuit of a dark blue Ford Focus." She gave the license plate number she'd written down out of the file. "The driver of the vehicle is a white male who may be armed and dangerous. We need assistance from marked units."

Five minutes later the radio crackled. The suspect had been pulled over, and Kyle Rossmoor was arrested and taken to the police department for questioning. Patty and Rick started back as soon as they heard the suspect was in custody and arrived at the station a few minutes later.

"We've got him in the interview room," Brad said as he stepped into the detectives' office.

"Thanks, Brad," Patty said.

"Good cop, bad cop?" Rick asked as he and Patty left their desks and started down the hall.

Patty nodded, to which Rick replied, "As usual?"

Patty smiled. "I'll be good cop. But let's let him stew for a while before we ask him anything. Maybe he'll give something up."

The detectives entered the interview room to find their suspect handcuffed to the metal ring embedded into the steel table. They each took a chair opposite Kyle. Behind them was a one-way window.

"Why am I here?" yelled Kyle.

"You evaded the police," Rick said.

"I just got scared. You had no right to pull me over."

"This would have been easier at your home," Rick said. "But it will be a long time before the word 'easy' is part of your life again."

The coloring on Kyle's face had turned a deep red as he kicked his legs around and jerked his hands away from the solid metal ring preventing him from moving his arms.

Patty and Rick glanced at each other and then sat quietly staring at Kyle.

"Well," he yelled, "you've got me here, so ask your questions." Not hearing from either of the detectives, he yelled again. "Look, I'm sorry I ran. I just got scared is all. So why not just let me go?"

The suspect didn't know what to do with another minute of silence as the detectives just sat and stared. Kyle quit thrashing about and sat still in the chair. "Okay," he said. "What is it you want?"

Patty glanced at Rick, nodded, and then sat back in her chair.

"You have the right to remain silent," Rick began. After admonishing the suspect, he leaned forward in his chair and stared into the eyes of Kyle Rossmoor.

"Why'd you do it?"

Kyle looked smugly at the detective. "Why'd I do what?"

"Kill Jonas Sorenson," Rick said. "Was it for money?"

Kyle slid down a bit in the chair. His eyes darted around the room and then settled up and to the right while he spoke, a motion many experts believe suggests the person speaking is either lying or making up what's being said. "First of all, I don't know who that guy is. And secondly, I didn't kill anyone."

"I think you did know Mr. Sorenson," Rick said. "You drove your mother to his home."

"I drive my mom a lot of places. I can't be expected to remember all of them."

"But you remember this one," Rick continued. "You sat outside for hours in that car of yours a couple houses down from Sorenson's place, watching his coming and going. "You've got the wrong guy," Kyle said, "and there's no way that you could prove that I or my car was there."

"But we can," Rick said. "Do you know you have a taillight out?"

Kyle sat up in his chair and furrowed his brow. "No, I don't," he said.

Patty sat forward and spoke softly. "Yes, Kyle, you do. And because there were times you sat in your car watching Sorenson's house in the evenings, the faulty taillight was noticed. Now, why don't you just tell us why you were out there?"

The color seemed to fade from Kyle's face as he stared back and forth at the detectives. "I'm not answering any more of your questions," he said. "And I want an attorney."

Patty gave a nod to Rick and stood up. She picked up her file from the table and the two of them left the room.

"This elevates the suspect status of Kyle," Patty said.

"I agree, and I'm thinking we may find something in his house that supports our suspicions."

"I'll request the warrant," Patty said, "and we can hold Kyle on an evasion charge long enough to search his place."

"While you write up the request," said Rick, "I'm going to call the state lab and find out where we are in the queue. I'll let them know that we suspect ours is the second homicide by the same responsible. Maybe that will help."

"I'm going to let the LT know that we're requesting the search warrant," Patty said. "I'll ask too if he can help expedite our request with the state, given the circumstances of the homicide in Louisiana." Patty walked down the hall to find the lieutenant at his desk.

"Come in, O'Toole."

"Thanks, LT," Patty said, taking a seat. "We've interviewed Pearl's son and he's definitely hiding something. We suspect that it was him who sat in his car in front of Sorenson's house several times. We just don't know why yet. I'll write the affidavit for a search warrant when I get back to my desk, and we'll hold him here until Rick and I have seen his house. We'll ask the judge to issue the warrant based on our belief that Kyle's residence contains evidence of his involvement in Sorenson's murder."

"Are you and Starker thinking this guy might be your responsible?"

"Hard to say, LT. We're expecting we might find stolen property in his house, maybe the coin collection. But other than the coin collection, we've not thought of a motive this guy would have for murdering Sorenson."

"Given his past history," said the lieutenant, "murder would accelerate this guy's criminal actions but it's not unreasonable, considering his treatment of animals. He might not think twice about murder, especially if his mother and her boyfriend are on board with it. He give up anything?"

"No. He lawyered up when he realized we know about the non-working taillight and that it was him who watched Sorenson's house from his car several times."

The lieutenant nodded. "Shows his criminal experience. Anything else?"

"There is, LT," said Patty. "Is there a way you might be able to influence the state lab to bump up our request to have the rope tested?"

"I checked on that yesterday, and they're aware of our need, but they've got a number of cases that must take priority, such as those where a suspect is already in custody. Keep investigating, and when you have someone for the crime, I'll call the state lab again if you've not yet received your results."

"Okay, LT. I understand. Thank you."

"You're welcome, O'Toole. You two keep at it."

Patty returned to her desk and filled Rick in on her discussion with the lieutenant. "It will be a day before Kyle has an attorney assigned to him. Maybe we'll find something in his apartment."

"That would be helpful," said Rick, "since we don't have anything else. I've called several of the Goldline rope customers from stores on my list and made calls to a few more stores that sell climbing equipment. So far, there's nothing that suggests the buyers used the Goldline for anything other than climbing, and in every case they purchased a large number of items that I don't think would have been purchased by someone buying rope for a hanging."

Patty's cell phone rang, and caller ID told her it was Chief Todd. "O'Toole," she answered.

"Detective," he responded, "I believe our mutual suspect may be back in Arcadia."

Chapter 14

Patty sat up in her chair and pushed the speaker button on her phone. "Detective Starker is here, Chief, so I'm putting you on speakerphone. Why do you think Faires is in Arcadia?"

"Yesterday one of my officers said he saw Faires at the local grocery store. At least he's pretty sure it was Faires. The guy was wearing a sweatshirt with the hood up, and I can think of only one reason why he's back."

"You think he's coming for you?" Rick asked.

"That's the reason," said the chief. "I've sent out a BOLO to my officers to let me know if they see him again."

"He's apt to go to your home, Chief."

"I've already considered that, and I've sent my wife to her sister's house for the next couple of weeks."

"Chief," Rick said, "if one of your officers sees him again, could you have him followed so as to determine where he's staying? If he's at a local motel, the manager may be willing to give you the garbage out of Faires' room. You may find something with his DNA on it."

"Not necessary," said the chief.

Patty and Rick spoke in unison. "You have it?"

"It's with the state lab." Before Rick or Patty could ask more questions, the chief explained. "Louisiana is the only state with a law requiring police officers to provide genetic samples. The law was enacted in August of 2003 and has proved to be helpful with crimes in which the prints or DNA of crime-scene officers are picked up with those of the criminal."

"I had no idea," Patty said.

"Me neither," said Rick. "And it makes me wonder why all states don't have such a law."

"Unions," said the chief. "Union leaders say that management won't restrict how the DNA information is used and stored, and the unions caution officers about potential privacy and misuse problems."

"I understand the need for personal privacy rights," Rick said, "but there are ways to ensure that the DNA is not improperly accessed or stored. The benefits far outweigh the downside."

"I agree with you, Detective, but the unions are stronger than a few members of law enforcement who can attest to the benefits of the law. It's interesting to note that other parts of the world, including the United Kingdom and Australia, have been keeping officers' DNA on file for years."

Patty sat back in her chair. "So you have Faires' DNA. What a relief."

"I won't ask for it until we have reasonable evidence that he's guilty of one or both of the murders. With the right evidence, I'm sure the state lab can make it available soon after we submit a request."

"Thanks, Chief. This could be the break we need."

Patty ended the call, and she and Rick sat back in their chairs. "Faires showing up in Arcadia puts him in position again as the front-runner for the homicide," Patty said. Brad walked into the office and handed the detectives their search warrant for Kyle Rossmoor's apartment. "Just came in," he said.

"Thanks, Brad," Patty said as she and Rick got up to leave.

The detectives climbed into Rick's unmarked and drove to Kyle's apartment. Rick walked up to the door, knocked loudly, and demanded entrance to search. After a few minutes he knocked again. After another short wait, he used the key that was part of Kyle's personal effects held at the police department when he was locked up. "Police," Rick yelled when he opened the front door. "Anyone here?" All was quiet so the detectives stepped inside. Upon entering, they saw a sparsely furnished living area with a bedroom off to one side. Rick looked in the bedroom while Patty opened drawers and cupboards in the kitchen.

"In here, Rick," Patty called out.

Rick walked into the kitchen area and saw Patty looking into a large plastic garbage can. He glanced into the can. "Looks like the box Joseph Sorenson described that his brother used for the coin collection. I'll get a large evidence bag out of the car."

"This should keep Kyle locked up for a while," Patty said.

Rick agreed. "We need to find out if Kyle acted alone on the burglary or if his mother and her boyfriend Harold were accomplices."

"Let's start with talking to Pearl again," Patty said. "Maybe if she realizes her son could spend a lot more time in jail, she'll provide us with more information on the coin collection theft and whether it led to the murder of Jonas Sorenson." Patty used her cell phone to call the casino, and a woman answered.

"Casino restaurant. Are you calling for a reservation?"

"This is Detective O'Toole with the Brookings Police Department. I'd like to speak with your server, Pearl."

"Pearl's not in today, Detective. She called in sick this morning."

"Can you transfer me to the casino?" Patty asked.

"Sure, hold on."

Patty waited on the phone and listened to a combination of rock and pop music until a woman answered. "Lucky Seven Casino. May I help you?"

Patty introduced herself again. "I'd like to speak with Harold Bochner."

"I'm sorry, Detective. Mr. Bochner's vacation started today. He won't be back until next week."

Patty hung up the phone and let Rick know the outcome of her call. "I'm thinking they know we have Kyle."

"And," Rick said, "they know he's going to talk. Let's take a drive over to Pearl's place."

Before Patty could respond, her cell phone rang, and she could see that it was her mother. "Detective O'Toole," she answered.

"Hi, Patty, this is your mother."

Patty smiled, realizing her mother didn't think in terms of caller ID. "I'm pretty busy right now, Mom. Everything okay with you and Bill?"

"We're great, dear, and I won't keep you. Just want to extend a dinner invitation to you and Rick for next Sunday at our place. Becky's going to help me."

"Thanks, Mom. Let me talk with Rick and I'll get back with you."

"Great," Maggie said. "Bye now."

"Bye, Mom." Patty ended the call and then checked her file for addresses on both Pearl and Harold. When finished, she put her jacket on and headed out the door with Rick. "Let's stop by Pearl's and then go to Harold's if we don't find them there."

When the detectives pulled up at Pearl's trailer, they saw two cars parked in the driveway.

"How do you want to do this?" Rick asked.

"We'll let Pearl know that Kyle's in jail again and could use his mother's help. Maybe she'll agree to talk with us."

Rick stepped out of the car and, with a slight movement of his arm, felt the gun on his side. Patty walked ahead up the three metal stairs to the trailer door. She could hear music playing inside the trailer. She knocked loudly on the door and backed down two of the three steps.

A man yelled, "Who's there?"

"Police," Patty called out.

Thirty seconds later, Pearl opened the window curtains slightly, peeked out, and then disappeared. Another thirty seconds passed before the music was turned off and Pearl opened the door.

"What do you want?" she asked.

"We need to talk with you," Patty said. "Kyle's been arrested for evading a police officer."

Before Pearl responded, she heard a man's voice coming from inside the trailer. "That dumb kid! Can't stay out of trouble."

Pearl turned her face to the side, looking toward the back of the trailer. "I told you before, Harold, don't call him dumb. He just messes up sometimes."

Pearl then gave her attention back to Patty. "So he evaded the police. You can't hold him long for that."

"No," Patty said, "but we can for burglary."

Pearl stared at Patty as Harold walked up beside Pearl. Seeing this, Rick positioned himself beside Patty.

"What do you mean, burglary?" Pearl asked.

"We found a box in his apartment," Patty said. "It's the box Jonas Sorenson used to store his coin collection."

The pink tint they'd seen in Pearl's face when questioning her at the restaurant came back. Harold seemed unintentionally to take a step back.

"How would you know what the box looked like that Jonas stored his coins in?" Pearl asked. "You didn't see it in his house, and I didn't describe it to you."

"No," Patty said. "You didn't. But his brother did, and his brother will testify that the box in your son's apartment belonged to Jonas."

"That dumb kid," Harold yelled out again. "That's his problem, Pearl. Let's leave on our vacation."

Pearl began wringing her hands and fidgeting from one foot to the other. "There's nothing I can do," she said to Patty. "Kyle's been in trouble since he was a kid. He's not my problem anymore."

Patty reduced the number of steps by one between her and Pearl. "I'm afraid that's where you're wrong, Pearl. Finding the coin box in Kyle's apartment is your problem. It's also your problem, Mr. Bochner," Patty said, though he'd backed up out of sight. "Kyle will be told that he's going to prison for a long time, and his attorney's going to want to make a deal. We don't believe Kyle committed the burglary alone. He had to be shown where Jonas Sorenson lived and told about the coins. He's going to want to reduce his sentence as much as possible, and that will require his telling us about the role both of you played in the theft."

"Maybe not just the theft," Rick said, loud enough for Harold Bochner to hear. "Maybe also about your role in Jonas Sorenson's murder."

"I ain't murdered anyone," Harold said, walking again up to the front door.

He then looked at Pearl. "And your dumb kid's not throwing me under the bus."

Pearl looked at Harold. "Well, you were the one with the idea to have him steal the coins. I should never have mentioned I saw them."

"So," Harold yelled at Pearl, "now it's my fault your kid's in trouble. You told him about the coins, and it was you who had to have some extra cash. So now you're throwing me under the bus too!"

Patty looked at Rick and then back toward Pearl and Harold. "Look," she said. "We've not yet been notified that he's implicated both of you in the crime. Why don't you two come with Detective Starker and me back to our office where you can sign a statement telling us exactly what happened. It might help if you talk before Kyle does."

Harold looked at Pearl and Pearl at Harold. "I'll do it," he said. "I don't want that kid blaming me for stealing those coins. All I did was take him to a shop where I knew he could fence them, and the fence pretty much stole them from us. The little amount I got won't even pay my gas for a month."

"I'll go too," said Pearl, "but I don't want to do any time for it if I tell you what happened."

Patty and Rick ignored the look of expectation for an answer to her last comment. "We'll give you both a ride," Patty said. "But we'll need to put these on you first and we need to read you your rights." She and Rick pulled out their handcuffs.

The detectives turned Pearl and Harold over to Pete when they arrived at the station. "We've already admonished them," Patty said. "Take them into separate interview rooms." She and Rick then walked back to their office. "I figured," said Patty, "that admonishing them back at the trailer was the best time to do so."

Rick agreed. "They were in a mood to cooperate and may not think about what was included in Miranda, at least not until they've given us what we need."

Patty sat down at her desk and glanced at her calendar. "Before we discuss how to proceed with our interviews, Mom asked if you and I can join her and

Bill for dinner Sunday evening at five. Becky will be there too, helping with the dinner."

"Great! It will be good to see them and learn more about how Bill's doing. Ask what I can bring."

"Okay. I'll take care of that now so I don't forget," Patty said, texting her mother. When done, she looked up at Rick. "Who do you want to talk to first?"

"Let's talk first with Pearl. We know that Bochner is only going to lawyer up after he blames Pearl and Kyle."

"That works for me," Patty said. "I'll be good cop to your bad."

"For a change?" Rick asked with a smile.

Patty shrugged as they left their office for the interview with Pearl. Walking into the interview room, they saw Pearl slouched back in her chair with her hands handcuffed and secured to the metal ring that was an integral part of the table. "Hello again, Pearl," Patty said as she and Rick sat down opposite the angry woman.

"I already told you back at the trailer what happened. I did mention to Kyle and Harold about seeing the coins, but I had nothing to do with stealing them."

Rick sat forward. "You mentioned seeing the coins to Harold? When?"

"What do you mean, when?" she asked.

"I mean did you tell Harold and Kyle about the coins after the first time you visited Jonas in his house?"

Patty knew where Rick was going with his questions. This brought a whole new picture to the relationship between Pearl and Jonas.

"I guess so," Pearl said.

Rick looked at Patty, who picked up the questioning. "So the three of you set up Jonas Sorenson. You didn't see him again because you liked him. You saw him to prepare for the theft of his coins."

Pearl no longer had the innocent appearance she had donned when they first spoke with her in the restaurant. Now she sat up and leaned forward on the table.

"So what if I did? Harold has to know where I am at all times, and he became suspicious the first time I spent the evening with Jonas. He would have killed me if he'd thought I was seeing someone else because I liked him. I had to tell Harold about the coins. I told him that Jonas came into the restaurant frequently and always wanted to talk with me. One time he mentioned his coin collection. I told Harold I figured it was a chance for us to make some big money. Of course, I didn't know what it was worth. What a waste of time when we got so little for it."

Patty sat back in the chair and Rick took over. "So you got your kid to sit in his car down the street from Sorenson's place and keep track of the time each day when the man was usually gone. What kind of a mother involves her son in a crime?"

Pearl pounded her fist on the table and gritted her teeth. "Don't badmouth me as a mother. I never wanted the kid anyway, and his father beat both of us. The first time Kyle went to juvie I split. How would I know the kid would find me? Now he's ruining my life again."

Rick didn't let up. "Whose idea was it to kill Sorenson? You must have figured that he'd suspect you for the theft of his coins. You couldn't have that, could you? Then you had your son and boyfriend do what you didn't have the muscle to do."

Pearl attempted to stand up, which was difficult with her hands secured. "I had nothing to do with his death! I didn't care if he thought I'd stolen the coins 'cause I would have lied and told him it wasn't me. I wasn't going to see him again anyway."

"You told your son to kill Sorenson," said Rick, "and then told your boyfriend to hang him from the tree. You're going away for a long, long time."

"I had nothing to do with anybody getting killed," Pearl screamed. "You told us to come to the police station because of the theft. Now you want to pin a murder on me. I'm not saying anything else."

Rick sat back in his chair and glanced at Patty, who folded her hands on top of the table. "I understand how difficult this must be for you, Pearl. If you really had nothing to do with the murder, we can't help you unless you tell us the truth. You know that Kyle and Harold are going to protect themselves. You need to tell us how they were involved, Pearl."

Pearl scrunched back down in her chair. "I don't know if they did it or not, and they're lying if they tell you that I was involved. Now, I want an attorney."

Patty and Rick closed the files in front of them, stood up, and left the room. Patty let the jail officer know that Pearl could be taken to a cell. Then they walked down the hall to the second interview room, entered, and found Harold cuffed to the metal table ring. He looked up at the detectives and then back down.

"Hello again, Mr. Bochner," Patty said. Harold remained silent, staring down at the table in front of him. Patty continued, "We just spoke with Pearl and she explained everything to us. It seems you'll be spending a lot of time behind bars. In fact, you may never have another birthday outside of prison."

"I had nothing to do with the guy's murder," he said. "If Pearl told you I did then she's lying."

"Let's start with the burglary," Rick said.

"I told you I only helped Kyle fence the coins."

"No," Rick replied. "You didn't like it much when Pearl was getting friendly with Jonas, did you? You threatened Pearl and that's when she told you about the coin collection. Your involvement didn't occur after the coins were stolen. You helped plan the burglary."

Harold fidgeted in his seat and looked toward one side of the room, the ceiling, and then the opposite wall, as if doing so would help him get out of the mess he was in. "Pearl wouldn't tell you that. She knows how mad it would make me."

Rick leaned back and Patty spoke quietly to Harold. "I'm sorry, Harold, but Pearl did tell us that. She told us that you planned the burglary and told Kyle what he was to do. You told him to sit outside Sorenson's house to determine the best time to break in with the least chance of Sorenson being home."

"You can't prove any of that," Harold said.

"Maybe not," Patty said. "But if Kyle backs up his mother's story, it's going to be two against one, and you'll lose. Your best bet is to tell us the truth, Harold."

Harold clammed up, and Rick waited a couple minutes before coming back at him. "You knew that Sorenson would side with Pearl if she told him she had nothing to do with the burglary. You knew you'd be found guilty, and you'd be the one to pay for the crime. So you did the only thing you could do. You killed Jonas Sorenson."

Harold Bochner looked up at Rick. "I want an attorney."

The detectives got up and left the room, giving instruction to have all three suspects transferred to the county jail in Gold Beach. Brookings' police department didn't have accommodations for anything other than short-term stays while being interviewed. All three were to be kept separated, each in a cell of their own.

Patty and Rick walked back to their office. "I don't know about you," she said, "but I'm exhausted."

"Me too," Rick said. "How about we call it a night."

CHAPTER 15

The next day both detectives were in the office early, each at their desk reviewing files, writing reports, and drinking their first cup of coffee for the day. One of the patrol officers stopped at the door. "Party in the break room in fifteen minutes. Pete's wife has given birth to their fifth! He thinks he's coming to work to pick up an important file the lieutenant said he needs for Pete to review at home. Patrol bought a cake and I brought some premium coffee."

"I knew with my first sip that this wasn't our usual coffee," Patty said. "It has a much richer taste."

The officer smiled. "I think so too. It's from Bayside Coffee in Charleston. See you in fifteen."

"We'll be there," Rick and Patty said in unison before the officer went on down the hall.

"Wow!" Patty said. "I can't imagine having five kids. Taking care of them when they're babies and toddlers is fun, but they have emotional needs when they begin to mature. How does a parent find the time to spend on each individual kid?"

Rick laughed. "Being the mother of an only child, I imagine you spend a lot more time meeting Becky's emotional needs than most parents who have more than one child. I was one of seven and I don't think meeting the emotional needs of each of us was on my parents' agenda. All in all, I think I turned out okay."

"You turned out great, Rick. But as a parent I would want to have time for each individual child. I couldn't do that and work full-time too if I had more than one child."

Rick smiled at Patty. "Have you thought about having more children someday?"

"Oh sure," Patty said. "I would like to have had more, but the way things turned out, I don't expect it will happen. I'm thirty-eight. Almost too old to think about having another child. How about you? Do you think about having more children?"

"Not at all for the first couple of years after Claire and Skylar died. But I'd like to have a relationship some day that's close enough to lead to marriage, and if I do, I'd like to have more kids."

Patty turned her head at an angle. "How many more?"

Rick laughed. "Well, not five!"

Rick looked into Patty's eyes and neither said anything. Then his phone rang, bringing them both abruptly back to the job. "Starker," he said.

"Detective Starker, this is Sam Potts. I manage the Upscale Climbing store in New Orleans. You called about a week ago asking if anyone had come in shopping for Goldline rope."

Rick quickly found the file on his desk and opened it to the list of businesses he'd called. "Yes, Mr. Potts. I remember talking with you. I believe you were going to check receipts over the past couple of years. Did you find something?"

"Well, I'm not done checking my receipts, however, I did have someone come in today asking about Goldline. It was kind of strange."

"Did he say why he wanted it?" Rick asked.

"No. For a while I didn't think he was going to buy anything. He kept talking about the cabin he rents. He said the owner had been in the Navy and later got into climbing. Said the owner stores his equipment in a barn on the property and that's how he discovered Goldline rope. He just wanted to know if I carried it and if there was a minimum amount he had to buy."

"What did you tell him?" Rick asked.

"I let him know that I would require a minimum of one hundred feet because I'd have to order it."

"Did he place an order?" Rick asked.

"That's what was strange. After talking for close to an hour he placed an order for the minimum."

"Did he pay for it today?"

"I only asked for a small down payment which he gave me in cash."

"Did you get his name?

"No, I'm sorry, Detective, but he never gave his name."

"What did he look like?" Rick asked.

"Well, he was about five-eight, not a tall guy, and bald. I'd guess he was in his mid-thirties. He wore jeans and a sweatshirt."

"Glasses?" Rick asked.

"No."

"Will he be picking up the rope when you have it or did he ask you to mail it to him?'

"Said he'd pick it up here."

"Did he give you a phone number to call when the rope comes in?"

"No. I called my supplier and was able to tell the customer it would be here in three to five days."

"Okay," said Rick. "I appreciate the call. Please call me again when the rope comes in."

"No problem," said Potts.

Rick filled Patty in on the call. "We need to let Chief Todd know about this."

Patty nodded. "While you call Todd, I'll talk with the LT."

The lieutenant was in when Patty walked up to the door.

"What have you got, O'Toole?" he asked.

Patty sat down. "Rick just got a call from a store in New Orleans that sells climbing equipment. A man walked into the store this morning and ordered one hundred feet of Goldline rope. He boasted of finding a lot of climbing gear in a cabin he rents. Said the gear, including the Goldline, belongs to the owner."

"You let Chief Todd know?" asked the lieutenant.

"Rick's calling him now," said Patty. "Rick also asked the store owner to let us know when the rope comes in."

"That's good," said the lieutenant. "If it's Faires, he may be getting a bit sloppy."

"The store owner gave a description but said the man who came in was bald. Faires has a full head of hair unless he's shaved his head."

"Rick should ask the chief if one of his officers can visit the store owner with a photo of Faires. We have a computer program here that can alter a photo. If Arcadia doesn't have such a program, offer to send the chief a photo of what Faires would look like without hair."

"I'll let Rick know when I get back to the office."

The lieutenant could see Patty's furrowed brows and the strained look on her face.

"What is it, O'Toole?" he asked.

"Well, LT, I'm concerned that even if Arcadia confirms that the man purchasing the rope is Faires, we have nothing concrete that says he committed the murder. He could say he's purchasing the rope for any number of reasons. If he's our responsible, we need something that ties him to one of the two hangings, and we've got nothing right now."

"You still haven't heard from the state crime lab?" said the lieutenant.

"No, we haven't, but even that's a stretch. If the killer wore gloves and left none of his or her own blood, how can the crime lab possibly come up with something we can use to convict someone? The ground cover was so thick around the tree that was used, it would be nearly impossible to find a useable shoe print. And as smart as this guy seems to be, he probably wore CS booties."

The lieutenant shifted in his chair. "What about your other suspects? Find anything more about their involvement with the burglary and murder?"

"We did. All three are being transported to Gold Beach as we speak. The mother, Pearl, turned out to be a real hard-core case. She blames the burglary on her son Kyle and the boyfriend, Harold. Said Harold found out about her time spent talking to Sorenson at the restaurant and then going to his house. According to her, she told Harold about the coins out of fear. She said Harold then masterminded the crime, and she told Kyle to sit out front of Sorenson's house monitoring his coming and going."

"How did you and Rick read her?"

"We kept at her, not sure if there was more, and there was. Turns out she told Harold about the coins after her first visit to Sorenson's house. They'd already planned to burglarize him when Pearl was there a second time under the guise of liking Sorenson."

"You ask about the murder?"

"We did, and she denies having anything to do with it. She didn't rule out Harold and Kyle committing the crime."

"What about the boyfriend? Did he talk?"

"Not as much as Pearl. At first, he denied knowing anything about the coins. Then we brought up Pearl's admission about the two of them making plans after Pearl's first visit to Sorenson's house. He lawyered up as soon as we suggested his reason for wanting Sorenson dead."

"Keep digging," said the lieutenant. "You're a lot closer now than you were even a week ago. You and Rick will figure this out."

"Thanks, LT. We plan to keep at it," she said before leaving to go back to her desk. Finding Rick off the phone, she inquired about his call to Chief Todd. "Were you able to talk with the chief?"

"I did, and he was happy to get the information. He and his officers are staying alert on the BOLO for Faires."

"Well," said Patty, "there's nothing much we can do for a few days with Pearl, Harold, and Kyle locked up. This would probably be a good time to work on a couple of reports that have been on my desk for the past week."

"I've got the same idea," said Rick. "Except I think I'm going to need another piece of Pete's congratulatory cake before I start writing." He stood up. "I noticed a while ago that there's plenty left. You want a piece?"

"Thanks," said Patty. "Think I'll pass. We've got dinner at Mom and Bill's place Sunday and I find I have to lose a couple pounds before eating at their place because that's what I seem to gain after their five-course meals."

"That's interesting," Rick said. "I also prepare for your mom and Bill's dinners. I find if I increase my consumption of food and gain a couple pounds before eating at their place, their multi-course meals have no effect."

Patty shook her head. "Go get your cake," she said, laughing as Rick left the room.

The afternoon came and went, as did Friday, with little action as the detectives worked on reports and returned phone calls.

Chapter 16

Sunday evening Maggie and Bill held their dinner party.

"Hello, Rick," Bill greeted him, opening the front door. "So glad you could make it."

"I wouldn't miss an opportunity to visit with you and Maggie," Rick said. "You look great. How are you feeling?"

"I'm still sore after the surgery and pretty tired, but other than that I'm doing okay."

"Good to see you, Rick," Maggie said as she walked up and gave him a big hug. "We're so pleased that you could join us."

Rick hugged Maggie back and then handed her a bouquet of flowers. "Great to be here. Thanks for the invitation."

"Rick's been preparing two days for this meal," Patty said, laughing as she walked in from the living room.

"Preparing for two days?" Bill asked.

"It's an office joke," Patty said. "We have both mentioned how much we love your and Mom's cooking."

Bill smiled. "Well, come into the living room where we can all sit down."

As Rick walked toward the couch Becky walked up to him and gave him a hug. "Hey, Rick. How's the murder case?"

"Hey, back atcha, Becky. Your mom and I should have the responsible found, tried, and convicted by this time next week."

Becky laughed. "Doesn't surprise me. What would you like to drink? We've got white, red, and beer."

"A beer would be great," Rick said. "The bottle's fine."

Patty looked at her mom and Bill. "Bill's had surgery and you've both taken a cruise since Rick and I've seen you. Do you want to tell us about your surgery, Bill?"

"I was out during the surgery so all I can tell you is that it went well and that I'm going to be sore for a while. Now I'd like to let your mom talk about the cruise."

Maggie looked at Bill. "It was great! Only a short cruise but long enough for Bill to win the fare!"

"That's amazing," Rick said. "I can't win at solitaire and you're winning playing world-class poker. How do you do it?"

"Like anything," Bill said with a smile. "It requires practice and I've been practicing a long time."

Maggie took Bill's hand. "We've decided to go to the Bahamas in the Spring."

"That should be fun," said Becky. "Are the Bahamas a territory of the United States? Will you need a passport to visit?"

"The Bahamas," Maggie said, "are an independent country. Bill and I will carry our passports because, although they're not necessary for us to enter the Bahamas, we will need them to get back into the United States."

Oscar got up from his bed in the corner on the floor, ran over, and jumped into Bill's lap. "Hello, little guy," he said, scratching Oscar on the back.

"Poor Oscar seemed to really miss us this time," Maggie said. "The first day we were back home he wouldn't let Bill put him down. Tom takes good care of him, but his mind seemed a bit preoccupied when we gave him Oscar the night before we left. He was preparing to leave on a trip the day after our arrival home." Maggie looked at her watch. "Let's all move into the dining room where we'll begin dinner with clam chowder and a berry and nut salad. "That sounds great," Patty said, getting up. "This looks new, Mom." She picked up a glass ornament of a streetcar off an end table.

"That is new," Maggie said. "That's a replica of the Streetcar Named Desire that sits in New Orleans. New Orleans is where Tom went on his vacation this past week. Isn't it beautiful?"

Patty and Rick looked at each other, and Patty set the glass ornament back down. "It is quite pretty, Mom," Patty said. "Very thoughtful of Tom to bring it back for you." Patty looked at Rick. "Don't you think so?"

"I do. Did Tom say why he went to New Orleans?"

Maggie looked at Bill who shrugged. "He didn't say anything to me."

"I'm embarrassed to say that, with so much on my mind concerning Bill's surgery, I didn't ask. We'll have to ask the next time we see him."

"How long has he been your neighbor?" Rick asked.

"Two, maybe three years," said Maggie. "Hard to remember when he moved in."

"How did you meet him?" Patty asked.

Maggie and Bill looked at each other with a puzzled look on their faces before Maggie responded. "It was at the Manley Art Center."

"Yes," said Bill. "I recall now that it was during a Saturday Art Walk and we were taking in the beautiful art hanging at the Center."

"Did you know," Maggie said directing her question to Patty and Rick, "that Manley Art Center changes their art out monthly, and they have a classroom where members can learn all kinds of art?"

Patty smiled at her mother. "That's really nice, Mom. I'll make a point to stop in. So, you and Bill met Tom there?"

"Oh, yes, we had all stopped to admire the same painting. It was the artist's rendition of the new police station. When I saw that Tom was interested, I asked if he was in law enforcement."

"How did he respond?" Rick asked.

"As I recall," said Bill, "he said no and asked the same question of us." Bill looked at Patty. "That's when your mother proudly announced she was the mother of a detective here in Brookings."

"And that was before he became your neighbor?" Rick said.

"Oh, yes," said Maggie. "Though it wasn't long before he moved into this development. We recognized him as he moved his furnishings in, and we have all been friends since."

"I don't know about the rest of you," Becky said, "but I'm hungry. How about I say prayers so that we can eat the chowder while it's still hot."

"Good idea, Becky," said Bill.

* * *

When the evening was over, Rick offered to walk Patty to her car.

"It's got to be a coincidence," Patty said. "Don't you think?"

"Well," said Rick, "after twenty years in law enforcement, I don't really believe in coincidences. I say we both go home, get some sleep, and discuss it at the office tomorrow."

"Good idea," said Patty. "I'll think better in the morning."

Chapter 17

Monday morning the detectives arrived early, eager to continue the prior evening's conversation. Rick came in bearing a bakery bag. He pulled out a bacon-topped maple bar and tilted the bag toward Patty.

"Thanks," she said, taking out a chocolate old-fashion doughnut. "There's nothing like a good doughnut to start off Monday morning. I'll get coffee for us."

Rick handed his mug to Patty, sat back in his chair, and took a large bite of his pastry. Patty returned a couple minutes later and saw Rick wiping off his fingers with a napkin. "You're done?"

"Don't worry. I've got a second one in here so that you don't have to eat alone."

Patty smiled, took a bite of her doughnut, and sat back in her chair. "You start," she said. "What are your thoughts about Tom?"

"All we know is that he met your mom and Bill at a local event where he was admiring art, including a painting of the new police station."

"And," said Patty, "he was in New Orleans last week, which happens to be the same week your climbing equipment store manager reported someone coming in and purchasing one hundred feet of Goldline rope."

"We don't want to scare your mom and Bill, but you could show them a photo of Faires and ask if he resembles Tom."

"I'll do that," Patty said. "Though Faires might not look like the photo we have from the Arcadia police department. Did Chief Todd respond yet on whether they have the ability to show Faires without hair? If not, let's put the photo into our system so that we have it."

"I'll send him an email and ask," said Rick.

"It's really creepy," Patty said, "to think there's even a possibility that Faires could be living so close to my mom and Bill, and that he's been taking care of Oscar."

"I understand," said Rick. "But it's not likely, so let's get the two photos together and you can figure out how to show them to your mom without setting off alarms."

Patty's desk phone rang. "O'Toole," she answered.

"Detective O'Toole, this is Scott Prance, the attorney for Kyle and his mother, Pearl. They are willing to tell you everything about the burglary if we can make a deal."

"Go on," said Patty.

"It was Harold Bochner's idea to steal Sorenson's coin collection once he learned about it from Pearl. Bochner threatened Pearl and her son with bodily harm if they didn't go along with his plan. Pearl feared for her life."

"And you want?" Patty asked.

"Pearl will admit to being an accomplice to first-degree burglary if she serves only probation with no fine. Kyle will admit to actually stealing the coins and first-degree burglary for the minimum sentence and no fine."

Everything was quiet at Patty's end of the call so the attorney spoke up. "That's it," he said. "What do you think?"

"Well, you haven't mentioned anything about the murder charges."

"They've both been clear about having nothing to do with the victim's death, and you've got nothing that suggests they do."

"We're still waiting on evidence with the state lab," Patty said. "And then there's Harold. I'm guessing he'll have plenty to say."

"Well, our offer to talk won't last forever, Detective. You talk with your partner and let me know if you want the kingpin of the crime to do more than a couple years of time."

"I've made note of your offer, Mr. Prance. I'll discuss it with my partner and the DA and get back with you."

Rick heard Patty's side of the conversation and waited to hear what had been offered. Patty went through her notes on what the attorney was asking on both suspects. "There's no way," said Patty, "that we're going to accept this, and I'd like to go for the maximum sentence."

"No argument from me," Rick said. "Considering the crimes Kyle has committed, society would be better served if he were locked up for life. Pearl doesn't have the record her son has, but she certainly doesn't seem to think he has a problem, which leads me to believe she was a big problem during his early years."

"We don't have any solid evidence yet," Patty said, "to implicate any of them in the murder. But I don't want to eliminate them as suspects until after we've spoken to Harold and gotten our DNA report back on the rope."

"There's an email here from Chief Todd," Rick said, "and he's attached a photo of what Faires looks like without hair. I'll send it off to my New Orleans store manager and get confirmation on whether it could have been Faires buying the rope."

"While you do that, I'll go talk with the LT about the deal being offered for Pearl and Kyle."

The lieutenant was on the phone when Patty walked up to his office, but he waved her in. Once off the phone he gave her his attention. She explained the offer described by Scott Prance for Pearl and Kyle, and the thoughts she and Rick had on the case.

"I agree with you and Rick," said the lieutenant. "These are bad people. The maximum sentence may not be enough, but at least it will keep them off the street for a while. Talk to the DA and see what he thinks. Have you heard from Bochner's attorney?"

"Not yet, but we expect he'll call wanting a deal too."

"Most likely," said the lieutenant. "Any more on Faires?"

"Only that we now have a computer-modified photo of him with no hair. Rick is sending it off to the store manager in New Orleans where the Goldline rope was ordered, hoping to get an ID."

"Good work," said the lieutenant. "Anything else?"

"Well, LT, there is one more thing. It may not be anything, but my mom and Bill have this neighbor…" Before Patty could continue, Rick knocked at the lieutenant's door.

"The store manager who sold the Goldline rope called. The rope came in over the weekend and the man who ordered it just picked it up. The manager had read my email just before the guy came into the store asking about the rope. He's sure it's Faires."

"I'll call Chief Todd and let him know," Patty said as she got up to leave. "Thanks, LT."

The lieutenant nodded, and Patty and Rick returned to their office. "He's got to be taking Interstate Ten since it's the fastest route," Patty said. "That means he'll be in Arcadia in about five hours."

"With the rope," Rick added as Patty picked up the phone to call Chief Todd.

Only a few more hours and my plan will be complete. I've waited five years for this to come to fruition and I've found the chase exhilarating. Let me think: there's been one of me and how many of you? I've created one cold case after another as you all scratch your heads in awe of what I've been able to do. You could have had my superior abilities working for you had you understood all that I have to offer. But you couldn't recognize genius when I offered myself. Now who's the smartest? The only concern I'll have after taking care of you, Chief Todd, is planning my next move. I'd best not wait too long as I don't like to be dormant. Where do I go next?

After alerting the chief to the status of Faires' rope purchase, Patty began listening to several voice messages. She quickly transferred the first two to Dispatch for Patrol to handle. The third message caught her breath, and she looked up at Rick who was jotting down information from his voicemails. Rick set the receiver back onto the phone cradle.

"That was the state lab and they've got something for us," she said, barely able to control her excitement.

"How? What?" Rick asked.

"Let's find out," she said, pushing the speaker button.

"This is Detective O'Toole with the Brookings Police Department," she said. "I'm responding to a voicemail message left me from a Judy Plum about a piece of rope your lab tested for us."

"I'm Judy, Detective. I just put the file away. Hold on." Thirty seconds later Judy Plum was back on the phone. "I've got the file. We were able to get a DNA sample for you."

"DNA?" Rick said with surprise. "This is Detective Starker, and we saw no blood on the rope."

"You saw correctly, Detective. There was no blood on the rope."

"Then how?" Patty started to ask.

"We tested the rope for touch DNA, which could likely come from sweat."

"Sweat?" Rick exclaimed.

"That's right, Detective. Whoever pushed the noose over the head of your victim must have had a difficult time, causing him to perspire, and sweat, probably from his forehead, dripped onto the rope."

Patty and Rick looked at each other. "Wow," Patty said into the phone receiver. "That's amazing. Thank you so much for your testing. This should make our case! When will we receive the write-up on the test results?"

"I've asked my assistant to send them over to you today, Detective. Call me back if you don't receive them."

"I'll do that," Patty said. "Thank you again."

Once the call was finished, Patty asked Rick to call Chief Todd. "Tell him we'll be emailing the DNA test results from our lab to be compared with the DNA sample taken when Faires worked for Arcadia PD. Ask him how long it will take to let us know if it's a match and whether he can expedite the process. I'll go let the LT know."

Patty nearly ran into the lieutenant's office. He looked up and suggested she take a seat.

"Sit down, O'Toole. Good news?"

"You won't believe this, LT," said Patty, short of breath. "The responsible dripped perspiration on the rope! The lab has his DNA!"

The lieutenant smiled. "He perspired on the rope? I look forward to learning more about this. What are you and Starker doing next?"

"Rick is calling Chief Todd to learn how quickly they can compare Faires' DNA to the DNA from the rope. Our lab says we'll have their test results before the end of today."

The lieutenant sat back in his chair. "So Faires should be in Arcadia within the next four to six hours. It's two o'clock and you'll have the Oregon state lab results before five. If Chief Todd can expedite things at his end, you may know tomorrow whether Faires killed Jonas Sorenson. This would give Chief Todd the green light to put a BOLO out on Faires and bring him in for murder."

"This is unbelievable, LT."

"I agree, O'Toole. Who'd have guessed that we'd bring Faires down because he dripped sweat on the rope? I'm sure it will be a surprise to him too! If the match is positive, Chief Todd should send the rope he has in his evidence room either to his lab or to you so that our lab can test it. Might be that he was also sweating when he killed Hal Grover."

"I'll talk with Chief Todd," said Patty.

"Good work on the part of you and Rick. It will be good to wrap this one up."

"Very good," Patty said with a smile as she stood up.

"Before you leave, O'Toole. You had started to tell me something about your mom and Bill and a neighbor? Is that something you still want to talk about?"

"It was nothing, LT. No longer important. But thank you for asking," she said as she left the lieutenant's office.

Rick was just hanging up the phone. "Chief Todd said he can have the results of a DNA comparison to us by the end of the day tomorrow if we can forward our lab results to him this afternoon. He's as excited as we are about closing in on Faires."

"There's not much we can do now but wait," Patty said. "I should pick up the rest of my voicemail messages."

"I'm going to look in the break room for something to eat," Rick said. "I get the feeling we won't have a planned lunch break today. Want me to get you something?"

"No, thanks," Patty said. "I'm too excited to eat."

When Rick walked back into the office, Patty was on the phone. "I've made note of what you want," she said. "I'll talk it over with Starker and the DA, but it's not going to happen. We've got two people who will swear that your client was the one who planned the burglary and threatened them if they didn't carry it out." Patty was quiet for another minute. "I'll let you know," she said before hanging up.

Rick leaned back in his chair. "Bochner's attorney, I presume."

"It was, and he says Bochner will admit to participating in the burglary by providing Kyle with contact information for the fence. In return, he wants a minimum sentence if he tells us about crimes Kyle committed for which he's not yet been accused. What do you think?"

"Well, I think Bochner should receive the maximum sentence allowed and I don't think it will be difficult getting that. However, I think it would also be helpful to know what he knows about Kyle's crimes. Might solve some outstanding cases. When you talk with the DA, ask if we can meet with Bochner and his attorney to ask a few direct questions without specifically promising him anything. Once we get the information, we're done."

"I like that, Rick. I'll schedule the meeting and you can lead the questioning."

"Don't tell me," Rick said with a smile. "I get to be the good cop."

"Not a chance," Patty said. "Same roles, just in reverse."

"You're a tough lead detective, Patty O'Toole."

Patty gave Rick a smile. "I'll try the DA now and discuss our thoughts on how to proceed."

Twenty minutes later Patty had completed her conversation with the DA.

"I heard enough to know he agrees," Rick said.

"On all three suspects," Patty said. "I'll call Scott Prance and tell him no deals. Then I'll schedule our meeting with Bochner and his attorney. Maybe our DNA results will come in by the time I've finished the calls."

Ninety minutes had passed and both detectives had their heads down, each writing a report, when Patty's computer pinged, letting her know a new email had come in.

"This is it, Rick. I'm forwarding the report to Chief Todd and sending you a copy. I'll call to let him know it's in his email."

Rick began reviewing the DNA test results and Patty called the chief.

"I've got it," he said. "I'll forward it to my lab and let you know tomorrow whether they've confirmed a match."

* * *

The next morning Patty arrived at the office and found Rick already at his desk. "How long have you been here?" she asked.

"About an hour. I know it probably won't be until this afternoon when we learn the results, but I want to be here when the news comes in."

"Me too," Patty said. "Oh, Mom called me last night. She ran into Tom while picking up her mail and thought to ask him why he took the trip to New Orleans."

"I'm guessing it wasn't to buy rope," Rick said.

"No, it wasn't. Seems he has a few cousins who live in south Louisiana and he went to a family reunion."

"Well, I'm glad you didn't have to show the photos to your mom. It might have raised suspicion."

"I don't know if it would have raised suspicion with Mom, but our questions at dinner made Becky suspicious. She asked me yesterday if Tom was in any kind of trouble."

"What did you tell her?"

"I told her he's not in any trouble that we know of. Someday I'll compliment her on being very perceptive."

Patty's cell phone rang, and caller ID showed the call was from Prairie Grove. Patty answered. "O'Toole."

"Detective, this is Chief Walker in Prairie Grove. You're not going to believe this! I'm calling because I've just learned of a fatal accident yesterday on Interstate Ten. A drunk driver crossed the center line and hit another car head-on. The drunk is in the ICU of a hospital in Alexandria. The driver of the car he hit was found dead at the scene. One of my officers happened to be travelling back home from a conference and saw the accident happen. He called 911 and identified the deceased by his driver's license. The fatality was Morten Faires."

Patty looked up at Rick and he could tell that Patty had just heard something remarkable. "Rick and I are waiting now to hear from Chief Todd about whether Faires' DNA is a match to the perspiration found on the rope used here in Brookings. I'll let you know as soon as we hear anything."

"Sweat on the rope?" the chief asked.

"Let me call you back to explain," Patty said. "You'll want to hear about it."

"Thanks, Detective. I look forward to it."

"Before you go," said Patty, "did your officer get an address off of Faires' driver's license?"

"Let me take a look at the report. Yes, he did. It's in Brookings."

Patty wrote down the address and ended the call with Chief Walker. She then called Brad. "I need, as fast as possible, for you to find out who owns the property and whether Faires is a legal tenant. If the owner is someone other than Faires, find out if he or she knows whether there's climbing equipment on the site."

Patty then called Chief Todd with the information on Faires.

"Well, that is something," the chief said. "Faires killed by a drunk driver."

"I guess this means you can relax, Chief," Patty said. "Call your wife and tell her to come home."

"I'll do that now, Detective."

Patty filled Rick in on the call and then stepped down the hall to inform the lieutenant about the accident. Fifteen minutes later, Rick stepped up to the lieutenant's door.

"Come in, Starker."

"Thanks, LT. Brad says Faires was renting from an out-of-state owner. I asked if there was any climbing equipment at the house and the owner replied in the affirmative. He'd been a climber when living out here and kept some of his equipment including Goldline rope and pitons."

"That's it," said the lieutenant. "A bag full of pitons, if used as a weapon, could easily knock someone out and leave a number of small gashes."

"It's all coming together," said Patty. Before she could go on, her cell phone rang and she looked at the caller ID. "It's Chief Todd," she said to her lieutenant.

"Take it," he said.

Patty accepted the call. "O'Toole."

"Detective O'Toole, this is Chief Todd again. No sooner did we end our conversation when the lab results came in."

"Yes, Chief?"

"It's a match!"

About the Author

G. A. Cockerham is a published author living on the Oregon coast with her husband, Bruce, and it's Oregon's coastal towns that provide the locations for her murder mystery series. She's authored several published books following her retirement as an investment advisor and insurance broker.

Bruce Cockerham, the author's technical consultant for the law enforcement theme, is a graduate of both the California Command College and the FBI National academy.

www.ingramcontent.com/pod-product-compliance
Lightning Source LLC
Chambersburg PA
CBHW071528100726
47908CB00004B/1323